Trans

Mónica Lavín
Translated by Dorothy Potter Snyder

Meaty Pleasures

katakana
editores

Meaty Pleasures
First Edition 2021

© Mónica Lavín

© Translation by Dorothy Potter Snyder

© Cover art by Karla Cuéllar

Editor: Michelle Rosen

© Published by katakana editores 2021
All rights reserved

The characters and events portrayed in this book are fictitious. Any similarity to real persons, living or dead, is coincidental and not intended by the author.

No part of this book may be reproduced, or stored in a retrieval system, or transmitted in any form or by any means, electronic, mechanical, photocopying, recording, or otherwise, without express written permission of the publisher.

ISBN: 978-1-7365650-3-2

KATAKANA EDITORES CORP.
Weston FL 33331
✉ katakanaeditores@gmail.com

This collection of short stories was curated by D.P. Snyder.

Previous versions of D.P. Snyder's translations of *Postprandial*, *What's There to Come Back to?* and *The Caretaker* were first published in *The Sewanee Review*, Volume CXXV, Number 2, Spring 2017.

The story currently entitled *Bolero*, which has never been published before in English, was originally published in Spanish as *La cintura equivocada*.

Table of Contents

Postprandial	9
You Never Know	17
Bolero	27
Roberto's Mouth	33
Thursdays	47
What's There to Come Back to?	53
Ladies Bar	59
Señora Lara	69
A Foreign Body	79
The Perfect Woman	89
The Caretaker	101
Meaty Pleasures	113

Postprandial

AT THE RESTAURANT, YOU LINGER IN FRONT OF THE LECTERN and examine the menu's offerings.

You note the décor, a high-tech bistro style that catches your eye. Its entrance opens onto the hotel's lobby. It's mid-afternoon, so there aren't any dinner guests to make uncomfortable when you peek inside. The waiters are busy putting out the place settings and flower arrangements.

In hotels, dinner service begins at six o'clock. At a table beneath a small lamp attached to the wall, a man catches sight of you and nods in greeting. You smile and feel a strong urge to leave, since you already had a look around, but he signals you with his hand to come closer. He appears to be the manager, with his navy-blue jacket and red tie. You say hello and tell him that the place is quite lovely, that you didn't know about it. We just remodeled it, he answers, and asks you to sit down. I came to get a gift from Larios, you say, hedging. He tells you it'll just take a few minutes, that he wants you to taste a few dishes, that everything's new, the menu, the chef. Faced with his calm smile and slate-blue eyes, you weakly tell him that you're not hungry. He reaches out his big hands—you take note of just how big they are—and he orders the waiter to bring a few sample dishes. You think, why not? You like to eat, and this man wants your opinion.

It's five o'clock, and the waiter sets down two wine glasses and pours a splash into the glass of the man in the blue jacket. He buries his nose in it, inhales, and then asks you if you wouldn't mind accompanying the tasting with some wine. It would be a pleasure, you say, and he explains what a good year it was for this French wine, the harvest of that vintage was fantastic, that this sort of Pinot Noir goes well with a tuna steak, a small slice of redfish, nearly raw and crusted with pepper, an intensely flavored slice that your tongue lingers over and that you swallow with your eyes half-closed, then taking a sip from your glass. He observes you, having not even tasted his own serving, and he catches you in your gesture, the look of satisfaction in your eyes, your sigh of pleasure. The servings—loin of lamb in puff pastry, a bit of endive with goat cheese, veal with morels—all flow delicately and each in its turn across the white tablecloth and your palate. He tells you that he used to be a dishwasher, and now he's the restaurant's manager. The story intrigues you. He's been to wine tastings all over the world, he personally knows sommeliers who have identified regions, varieties, and vintages while blindfolded.

He calls the waiter and asks him to straighten a painting on the wall and to fill up the saltshakers, his eyes focused all the while on the man's shoes—they must be perfectly polished at all times, he explains. His slate-blue eyes gaze at you steadily and with a certain enjoyment as you taste the Château Lafitte that the waiter has uncorked, and you observe and listen to him as if you were part of a play in which you had the role of submitting to the designs of the leading man. Finally, he offers you a serving of bitter chocolate on a small, white, seashell-shaped plate, and he assures you that it tastes best accompanied by champagne. So, he takes your hand in his big one, and he sweeps you along through the hallways while you discover that he's tall, and that you like his light chestnut hair and the way he carries himself, and you don't know whether it's his mixed French and Scottish ancestry or what you learned amidst the dishes, implements, tables, chefs, and waiters that is seducing you.

He takes you to Room 704, and you don't understand how the bottle of champagne got there first and is now reclining in a silver ice bucket. You sit on the sofa next to the bed and wait for him to offer you a glass while you silently observe through the window and from seven floors up this strange city and your own acquiescence. You feel out of place in this position. You smile, and he of the slate-blue eyes brings over the glass, and while you drink, he silently removes your shoes, unbuttons your blouse, and delicately searches for the center of each of your breasts to play with the nipple. Once again you half-close your eyes and you surrender yourself to the big hands that have just stripped you naked and that hold you there on the sofa with the afternoon sun streaming through the window, and the rug, and his long nose sniffing at your neck, and his champagne-flavored tongue savoring your breasts, sucking from them the secret of their whiteness. He sucks on your navel, nibbles your legs, drenches your feet with his saliva, and strokes your belly as if he were checking the freshness of a Dover sole. He observes the response of the flesh and searches with an artisan's hands for your throbbing clitoris. He stimulates it delicately, as if he were seasoning a dish that afterwards his mouth had to savor, his tongue to wound. You've turned to jelly: a jumble of moist flesh, a cream of cockles, a dripping sieve of spit and membranes. You're completely edible, and he's gotten you to the point where you want nothing more than to taste him, to feel his sex growing in your mouth, drowning you, leaving you breathless, exalting your desire that he should pierce you, break you down, and skewer you, as at last he does, leaving you limp and abandoned like leftovers on a plate.

You let a week pass. You needed time to enjoy the postprandial, and you thought that choosing the same day and time would allow for a repeat encounter. Before leaving home, you carefully polished your black shoes, and you drove there, all the while trying to ignore the feeling of inevitability. It could've been just the moment's enchantment, but nevertheless you had already drunk from the cup, and your body clamored for his mouth endlessly sucking on your breasts. It was five o'clock when he saw you walk in. As you approached, he stood up, his pale-yellow shirt peeking out from beneath his gray jacket. The two wine glasses were already on the table, waiting. Everything proceeded like a concert directed perfectly by his slate-blue eyes and expert hand, the hand that you were craving. The parade of food began, the snails bourguignon that he pried from their shells, trembling as if still alive when he placed them on your tongue, the garlic and oil providing lubrication. Later, he offered the Spanish Matarromera to soften the flavors and heighten the desires, which were then soothed with some oysters *al parmesano*. And a new appetite was born that would not be satisfied with any other tastes than those of skin and sweat in another and different room, with the same afternoon light and the tumult of his taking you right in front of the mirror while he observed your movements, your flushed skin, your wild eyes, and he grabbed onto your breasts like the peaches that he had chosen that very afternoon to infuse with wine and sugar. And you sought the source of this pleasure in his slate-blue eyes reflected there in the mirror, the duration of this pleasure that then became lost as the glass misted over with vapor from the bath.

You took refuge in the ritual, became an addict, relinquished your own ordinary good sense every Friday for months, between the wine and food and champagne that were like a prelude to the ever-new and wild carnal pleasures that required neither the soul's cooperation nor the reassurance that there would be an encore. That's how it was. That's how it was until the afternoon when his slate-blue gaze received you more somberly, and he reprimanded the waiter on duty for his scuffed shoes, and he sent back the saltshaker that had grease marks on it and said that the flowers' aroma spoiled the meal. There were dishes that you ate with a certain disquiet—words hadn't been the currency of exchange between the two of you—and he regarded you with a nostalgia foretold. He uncorked a Vega Sicilia that you finished on the eighteenth floor. Closer to heaven every time, you told him. In response, he made love to you with sweet frugality, he touched you delicately, kneeling next to the sofa in the blushing afternoon light and letting you drink from his glass. He absorbed your moisture so that he might leave you dry as a shell, and he rammed you up against the wall and entered you as if he were raping you in a dark alleyway, your anxious hands clawing the wall. He drew the bath while you looked out at the tranquility of the approaching darkness, unaware of the whirlwind that was also coming your way. He told you about it once you had lowered yourself into the tub, while he contemplated you there, your hair spread out on the surface of the water. *I am going to a hotel in Niza.* Speechless, you submerged, letting your face sink below the water. *When?* you asked when you finally resurfaced. *Tomorrow*, he said, *tomorrow afternoon*. *Why?* you asked him while he used a sponge to wash your foot, which was sticking out of the tub. *It's better work.* You looked at him, furious. *You should have stayed a dishwasher.* You wounded him, but he kept on following the contours of your skin, and then he took your leg and scrubbed it hard, his hands plunging into the water, rubbing your belly, your chest, your reddened nipples, and you, looking at his desperate face, pulled yourself together enough to embrace him, get him wet, kiss him, take the sponge away from him, and lower yourself down on him to make love on the bathroom floor, like one last, lacerating howl.

He was so kind as to recommend you. Perhaps, you thought, it was a way of prolonging the time that you had been his. He spoke with the owner about your gastronomic sophistication, your elegance, your taste buds, of the wines you knew and could recommend, and you said yes. It was a good job, and now you could sit at the table against the wall beneath the lamp, giving orders, inventing and distributing pleasures for others, keeping a close eye on the waiters' shoes. You watched him come in with his notebook, a young man who was writing an article for a magazine. Sit, you signaled to him with your hand, and you told the waiter to serve the parade of dishes and your preferred wines. The young man half closed his eyes while he savored a piece of salmon *aux fines herbes*, and you smiled. You gestured at the waiter. The champagne would be waiting for you in Room 704.

You Never Know

You never know whether one day you might get out of bed and Papá might also get up, looking all anxious and unshaven, and put your cereal on the table and your sisters might speak in low voices, nobody mentioning that Mamá isn't there anymore. You might go to school thinking you'll see her again, but it'll be Trini who opens the door of the apartment and she who serves the noodle soup and grumbles because from now on it's going to be up to her to take care of everything as if she were the lady of the house. You might think someone's going to throw something, file a complaint, ask a question, or break a dish, because a mother can't just take off like that. But instead, your sisters stroke your head, and Papá comes home in the evening and asks you about school and soccer, feigning interest. Sitting there on the edge of your bed, he has no clue that you haven't brushed your teeth, and he seems on the verge of explaining something to you, but when his eyes wander around the shelves covered with toy cars, he says a gruff goodnight. You never know whether silence might be the only explanation you get, or whether everyone might just go on living as if the absent mother's voice were smoke, as if on Sundays you'd always been just four at the dinner table, as if they sold socks with holes already in them, as if it were normal for Trini to take you to your doctor's appointment in a taxi. And you might go to school with eyes as big as plates, your disbelief gluing your lashes to your eyelids because nobody has dared to cry or kick the doors, and because the only conspicuous change is all the missing photographs. Only on Papá's nightstand is there still one in black and white where they are both sitting on a bench looking happy. Traces of your mother linger in that room where you almost never go, because it's better not to entertain dangerous thoughts about the size of the bed, the two pillows, or what's behind those closet doors. You don't even know if her dresses are still hanging in there because your sisters have taken charge of locking all her things up, and your sisters are the ones who now go to your school events, sign your report card, and speak with your teachers. Your silent father walks around the house like a backdrop, and you might figure that it's the only way he can handle the fact that there was no goodbye kiss.

You grow up, and you get used to grumpy Trini, to your sisters with their boyfriends in the darkened living room, to the family gatherings with your grandparents and the casual references to the mother's traits that have been reproduced in her children, comments as passing as a cloth sweeping dust off the furniture. You learn not to visit *abuela* Nona because all she ever talks about is Papá and his silences, and because her peevish sisters won't stand up to her or her never-ending search for the reason for her grandchildren's orphaned state. You don't want to be in other people's homes where you're reminded of a mother whose face is beginning to become hazy in your memory. The years go by, and you start noticing women's legs, and you imagine kissing them and petting them, and you'd give anything to put your arms around a slender waist and inhale some sweet breath. Then, you kiss and hug them in the shadows of a movie theater, and you masturbate thinking about them, and when you start to want something more than their bodies, like their companionship and tenderness, you leave without saying goodbye.

And that's how it happens that one day you can leave without an explanation. You overheard a furtive conversation between your father and his sister-in-law that somebody spotted her in New York City, that she's a waitress in a diner on Second Avenue. You think a joint like that must be full of cooking grease. And you screw your courage up. You're twenty-one, and you work in your uncle's law office while you're going to college, and you've saved enough money to spend a month in the city. So, you tell your father you're going to take a trip, and you don't say when or where. One day, you just take a plane, and it rises quickly into the air.

There are a great many diners on that long, long avenue. You rule out the Chinese restaurants, pizzerias and bars, but there are still many places she could be. You rent a room in a shabby hotel on 92nd Street and First Avenue. Your plan is to walk the length of both sides of Second Avenue, from the Lower East Side up to Spanish Harlem. You are sure you'll succeed. You have all the time in the world and enough money to buy tea, soft drinks and donuts, because it's not enough to look in from the street and you have to sit down inside. You have to be able to recognize her thirteen years after your last memory of her face, which won't look like the face in the photograph on your father's nightstand anymore.

You walk wearing sneakers and a heavy jacket because now, in April's waning days, a light rain or snow might take you by surprise. You don't talk to anyone and you don't find the solitude difficult. Two weeks pass and you've looked through the vaporous, greasy front windows of diners where the waitresses call you *dear*, and you've searched among the delicate, white place settings of the hotel dining rooms as well. You've gone into the same places both morning and evening, because who knows what shift a waitress might work in this city that never sleeps? Before leaving the hotel, you mark your chart and, like somebody going to the racetrack, you place your bets: return to Ruby's, walk from 40th Street to 60th Street. You plot your course by means of a combination of calculations and hunches. And that's how it happens that three weeks later, having managed to avoid becoming too morose in the evenings and with your hopes undimmed, you enter

You Never Know

the diner at the corner of Second Avenue and 95th Street and, as you fold up your chart and slip it into your pocket, you realize you've found her.

You watched her put down the plates on the next table, her beige-uniformed body leaning, and it was this very gesture, her way of clearing the used plates from the table, that gave her away. That sudden delivery to the dining room table. You'd thought it would be her gaze, her long neck, or maybe her sharp nose that would help you recognize her, not that domestic posture from so long ago that has now become an occupational hazard. You want to observe her like that from a distance, but she becomes aware that a customer is waiting. You hide behind your menu. You know that soon you'll hear her voice. You peek at her legs and her flat-heeled, rubber-soled shoes.

Good morning. Are you ready to order? she asks you in strange-sounding English.

You look at her because you're taken aback, because you want to regard her as if she were a photograph: the dyed ash-blonde hair, the sharp nose, the compulsory smile. She follows up with her next question.

What are we up for this morning?

You might not know what to do when your mother speaks to you in English while she pours reheated coffee into a chipped cup. So, before she can get away and leave to serve another table because this customer hasn't made up his mind yet, you order some pancakes just to keep her there. You realize that everyone is calling out to her, that she serves them, and that they leave small change for her on the table. You don't know what to do in the presence of a mother who doesn't display the least deference to this customer who is a part of herself but whom she regards with no greater interest than she does the workman at the next table, or the ladies in a booth in the back.

When she brings the steamy pancakes, his *thank you* betrays that he's from someplace else.

¿Visitando? she asks.

Buscando trabajo, you say brusquely as you spread pats of butter on your pancakes. Looking for work. You watch the heat liquefy them. You take pains to slice the circular cakes with your knife into equal-sized wedges. You don't know what's going to happen next. You chew and swallow them with difficulty, anxious to get out of that diner as quickly as possible. You gesture at your mother:

La cuenta. Check, please.

Accustomed to people in a hurry, the waitress leaves the check next to your sticky plate.

You take off walking and feel disoriented. You go to the corner and come back, cross to the other sidewalk, and then start walking along some street or another. Your hand brushes against the chart of the city in your pocket and you crumple it up, throwing it away in the first trashcan you find. But how can you waste this precious discovery? The night air has cleared your head. But you don't figure on her having a day off, and the next morning you don't see her in the restaurant. You walk up to a Black waitress. You ask for Olivia. It's her name and she hasn't changed it. The waitress answers that she'll be there again tomorrow.

One day seems like many years, the sum total of all the years since Trini started serving noodles to the three siblings eating all alone. Your anger mounts while your money dwindles. There's no time to lose.

The next day you go back, and you see her through the front window. You linger a moment to look at her tied-back hair and sharp nose. You sit at the same table as before, and Olivia—her name is written on the plastic name tag—asks you with a smile if you want pancakes again.

I came looking for you yesterday, Olivia, you say to her in Spanish.

Why beat around the bush?

It was my day off. Did you find work?

That's what I want to talk to you about. Would you have a drink with me tonight?

Olivia hesitates while she lays out the paper tablecloth and pours coffee in the cup.

I don't like coffee, you say.

She keeps filling the cup.

Five o'clock at the cocktail lounge, two blocks downtown, Olivia answers.

How much? You get up from the table.

But you haven't ordered anything!

It doesn't matter.

You leave a dollar on the table and walk out.

From early evening on, you drink at the cocktail lounge. Olivia walks over to you, standing very straight and looking taller now in her high-heeled shoes. She's wearing a long, navy-blue coat, her hair is down, and her bangs fall across her forehead.

I've never had drinks with such a young man.

I've never had drinks with a waitress in New York City, you answer. Are you Mexican?

You can tell? And you?

From El Salvador, but I went to college in Mexico, you lie.

They serve you vodka tonics, and you feel like talking as little as possible. You avoid asking about her life, but Olivia tells you she fell in love with a man and left everything behind in Mexico for him. You don't ask what happened after that, although you sense that she'd like to tell you how things turned out. But she keeps saying that she left everything for nothing, and just to make her stop talking, he caresses her leg. She goes quiet. You leave your hands on those thighs sheathed by the wool skirt to find out if you're able to bear this proximity to the woman's skin. She says nothing and just looks at you. You don't resist the familiar eyes. You grip your glass tightly so that you don't dash it to the floor. You order another round for both of you, and you feel as if she's surrendering when she accepts the drink. You leave together without any words passing between you, and you quickly guide her by the hand along the street, and you feel that she's as light as some little thing. You remember other bodies, and the feeling amazes you. As soon as you enter the room, you take off her coat and you push her down on her back, her hair fanning out on the sheet's dingy whiteness. You unbutton your pants quickly. Excited, Olivia takes off her stockings and panties. You enter her easily. You notice her flushed face and her eyes, which are closed, thank heavens. Then you think about how you're penetrating the same passageway that stretched wide open so that he could be born. You feel a lewd disgust and forget the words you had planned to say. Exhausted, you collapse onto her breast, and Olivia slides up to sitting position, looking for the cigarettes in her handbag on the nightstand. Your head is resting on those naked thighs, very close to her pubis. You don't want to look at her. You don't want to leave her sultry lap.

Olivia strokes your head with one hand while she raises the cigarette to her mouth with the other.

I hope this is a smoking room, she jokes.

You stay there with your eyelids squeezed shut, the silent truth frozen in your throat and your spent cock.

You have a sharp nose, too, says Olivia tenderly. Are you okay?

You cannot bring yourself to deliver the knockout punch. You do not say, Olivia Sansores, I am your son. Instead, you hide your sharp nose, smashing it desperately against the woman's leg. You end up falling asleep, hugging yourself. In the morning, you wake up alone. Your mother's scent lingers on the pillow, and you find the butt of her cigarette in the ashtray. You bathe so you can go back for pancakes. You find an empty table in Olivia's section. When she sees you there, she comes over to pour you coffee.

I told you. I don't like coffee. You cover the cup with your hand. Why did you leave?

I wasn't going to stick around till morning so you could see I'm forty-nine.

You wolf down your pancakes and leave all the money you have left on the table. That night, you take a return flight home. From the airplane window you see the illuminated grid of the city you're leaving behind and then the profile of your nose reflected in the glass. All you know is that it's better to leave without saying goodbye.

Bolero

The song cries its heart out to no avail against the distant murmur of the sea. Over and over, it repeats the rhythm and lyrics of the old bolero. *Viajera que vas, por cielo y por mar... Traveler who goes 'cross the sky and the sea...* Some people sing along with the lyrics, humming the melody. Floating above the song are the sounds of conversations and wine glasses clinking. No one dances on the terrace's glazed floor tiles. Someone says the steps for the *danzón* are very difficult. Ana stops following the beat of the music for a moment and says she'd like to learn it. Gabriel looks at her and continues humming the song in a low voice... *dejando en los corazones... leaving behind in hearts...* Ana dares to ask him, do you know all the lyrics? *It was my turn to love you, as well, to kiss you and then to lose you,* he sings by way of an answer. I like it, says Ana. But it's no use. The tune goes to waste as Gabriel's feet search out hers from where he is sitting and Ana's waist yearns for the support of a partner's hand in the small of her back. The two of them drink and gaze out at the thin line of white sea foam off in the distance.

Two couples have started to dance barefoot. Seaside vacations permit such informalities. The terrace of the house where they have gathered has become suffused with the placid, humid air of the coast and the well-being conferred by alcohol. Ana hadn't really felt like going to the beach with a bunch of strangers, but one of her mother's friends had invited them. Her mother almost never went anywhere, and Ana thought it would do her good.

Gabriel is a friend of the owner of this beach house in Jalisco. His wife is away visiting her parents in Lisbon, so he's there alone. Maga, the host's wife, insisted he come to enjoy himself this weekend when family and friends would be coming.

The waiting becomes painful. Two more couples start dancing. Ana also wants to, but she's not one of those women who is forward enough to ask men to dance. None of them inspire confidence in her, and what's more she wants the tall one with glasses to take her onto the dance floor, the one who knows the lyrics of the song and sneaks glances at her and laughs when their eyes meet just as she, too, is taking a quick peek at him.

Gabriel sees Ana's legs and thinks about how her body looks when she walks into the ocean alone. He talks with the others in the shade of the *palapas*, those rustic gazebos roofed with palm fronds, there by the seaside. But he doesn't dare to speak to Ana, who fascinates him. It's partly out of shyness and partly because he's a married man and here alone this weekend. He's not on the prowl for any flings. Of course, there's nothing wrong with speaking to a pretty woman, but he's afraid he'll want to continue the conversation on into the afternoon, through the sunset, and on into the next morning. That happens to him with certain kinds of women. So that's why he doesn't approach them, at least not in full view of a hundred eyewitnesses.

Mi luna y mi sol, irán tras de ti... My sun and my moon will follow in your footsteps... Somebody's pressed the repeat button, so that the bolero *Viajera* plays over and over again. Nobody seems to care. The dancers haven't stopped, and those who are chatting with each other continue to do so. Bit by bit, Ana and Gabriel join the conversations, without Gabriel once losing the beat of the music as he taps his fingers on his glass, and Ana looks every now and then at the people who are dancing.

Gabriel goes off to get himself another glass of wine and asks if anyone wants anything. No one answers. Ana waits for him to look directly at her. *Bring me a whisky, please.* When he returns, Gabriel holds out the drink and brushes Ana's fingers as they exchange glasses, the empty for the full. The situation makes them tense. Ana says a shy thank you, fragile and seductive. It's time for him to sit down next to Ana and talk. Everyone's talking. Ana feels comfortable with Gabriel next to her, and she no longer has to strain to catch snippets of conversation and make the occasional remark to keep from drifting away from the group, there between the terrace and the beach.

Maga in her beige polka-dot dress self-confidently asks Gabriel to dance. *It's my due as the hostess*, she says to Ana, as if begging her pardon.

Like a gentleman, Gabriel excuses himself and takes Maga by the waist. Ana should stand up now and tell him, you've chosen the wrong waist! Ana's gaze becomes lost between her drink that she's sipping too fast and the new couple on the dance floor. *No sé que será sin verte, no sé qué vendrá después... I don't know what will happen if I can't see you again, I don't know what will happen then...* Gabriel looks at Ana past the copper-colored hair of the hostess. Ana smiles softly, her expression seen only by the dancer who is holding the wrong waist and who, with a wry look, confirms that he knows it. After that complicit gesture, Ana can enjoy watching the couples. Gabriel dances well. Ana tries to imagine his scent, compares her height to his to triangulate how close her nose could get to Gabriel's long neck.

By the second repetition of the song, Ana becomes impatient. This is torture. She doesn't want to approach the group that's engaged in conversation just in case Gabriel reclaims the seat next to her. He does so, but this time, Maga comes along with him. She asks after Raquel and the children. When are they coming back? How you must miss her! But I'm sure you have no shortage of women admirers, she says. Uncomfortable, Ana goes to the ladies' room. The melody follows her... *the trembling of a song and later, a thousand disappointments...* She doesn't know whether perhaps it would be best for her to return to her room. They're leaving early tomorrow to go back to the city. When she exits the bathroom, she goes over to the bar and serves herself a soda. Gabriel comes over to pour himself another drink. Have you enjoyed the weekend? he asks to break the silence. Ana answers that she has, and they return to the table side by side, talking. Maga's no longer sitting where she was before. *It was my turn to love you, as well...*

Dance with me, Ana asks him suddenly. Gabriel's good breeding makes it impossible for him to say no. Then Ana's waist accepts the support of the hand that is leading her and the fingers that press firmly against her back. His rhythm on the glass and that of his feet on the earthen floor now are displayed harmoniously on the dance floor and he takes command of the space, pushing the distant murmur of the tide into the background. The other figures on the terrace melt away, and now the two of them are alone on the dance floor. The subtle fragrance of Gabriel's neck, the shoulder that seems to offer her shelter, Ana's hair gathered at the nape of her neck, her feet cleave to the steps that the man lays out for her as if they were a famous dance team.

They don't realize the song is on its third repetition, and the others have begun to stare at them. The music stops. Ana and Gabriel turn toward Maga, who is the one who turned it off and who now says it's time to let the others get some sleep. Ana and Gabriel look at each other sadly. Gabriel strokes Ana's hand.

How well you danced with me, she says.

I haven't stopped dancing with you all night, he answers.

Maga asks everyone to collect their glasses, and there's nothing else to do but obey and vanish down their separate hallways on their way to their separate bedrooms. Finally, it's Maga who turns off the terrace lights.

Their flight leaves early. Ana appears in the foyer with her mother and looks toward the empty terrace. She yearns to say goodbye. *My sun and my moon will follow in your footsteps...* She smiles.

It seems they've forgotten to turn off the music, her mother says, unaware that Gabriel, asleep in a chair on the terrace, is the one who has pressed *repeat.*

Roberto's Mouth

THE CITY WAS A QUILT OF LIGHTS SPREAD OUT BEFORE her, waiting. Ileana calmed her wild heartbeat with brushstrokes, coaxing the shine from her jet-black hair. She took a little mirror out of her purse, defined the outlines of her dark eyes and applied a peachy blush to her cheeks. When he saw the photo, he said he liked her cheeks. Ileana regarded them now, imagining his eyes traveling across her onscreen image. And I, your lips, she had written. Ileana held the mirror in front of her own lips now and applied a peachy color to them, too. In a few minutes, those faraway lips, those lips that had been only points of light on a screen, would be right there in front of her. Warm, they'd move when Roberto spoke, stretch wide when he smiled, soften and swell when he kissed her. They'd be moist and pink against her brown skin.

And what if the mouth on the screen wasn't Roberto's mouth? No, that couldn't be. Because then, he'd never have written *come to me* when she told him she was fed up, that she couldn't bear one more minute there with her husband, her kids, her mother-in-law, her mother, her life. What's more, it was afterward that the photo appeared, when she said yes, we'll see each other in the next couple of weeks, thinking how she'd take a taxi to the bus station as soon as her husband dropped her off at yoga class. How will I know it's you? she'd asked. Will you speak the same way you write? Will you see me from a distance and walk towards me, whispering that you can't wait to nibble on my neck, that you're getting excited even as you write the word neck, that you write to me inspired by your erection, that you could never before have imagined the power of words to make your body tremble with excitement, to make your pants bulge and become moist?

It was then that the photo arrived. It was only eight days ago that Ileana for the first time came to know the face of the man who'd been visiting her chat room every day for the past several months. She told him she lived with a lot of people and speaking with anyone privately was impossible for her. Her very young children made her happy sometimes, but that was it. Everything else was just tending to the house, her husband, the little ones, her figure, her parents, the kindergarten, the other mothers, the church and Sunday services, Sunday dinners with her mother-in-law and her sisters-in-law while the men played dominos. But what about her? Who knew what she thought, wanted, dreamed? Well, I do, Roberto wrote, soothing her. I know. Unbutton your pants and touch yourself. Imagine it's me. Imagine I know exactly where your dreams are. Your dreams are boiling rivers, and you abandon yourself to tides of undulating pleasure. You imagine that they turn you on, that they know you by touch, that they smell you and squeeze the loneliness out of you by sucking hard on your skin, by rubbing your nipples. I am your dream. I am the one who makes you lighter than air. And it was then that Ileana lost her mind. She discovered the language of desire. She exchanged her *I'm sad today* for *I was imagining that you penetrated me so hard I was pinned to the wall, that you left me bruised with pleasure, run through by your penis. I want you to hurt me.* Ileana hadn't known about the existence of magical words. The open sesame that banished her loneliness and discontent. *Openmeupagainandagain.* And they were real. Words had conspired to bring about this meeting. Though she hadn't said so to Roberto, Ileana was ready to leave everything behind for this language of salvation.

She took her exercise bag down from the overhead rack, tucked in her fitted blouse, smoothed her pants and, with the bag over one shoulder, she got off the bus. Now there was no way to slow her racing heart. As she passed through the turnstiles, she turned her head one way and then the other, searching for Roberto, of whom all she'd ever seen was his brown-skinned face, full lips, and dark slicked-back hair. She crept forward slowly, afraid of becoming lost among the throng of travelers. Slow and cautiously, like someone who wanted to be caught. She stood motionless in the center of the corridor, and then she saw him. Leaning against a pillar with his arms crossed across his chest, he was observing her. He smiled. Ileana froze. And if he wasn't Roberto? And if he was, why had he been watching instead of running over to greet her? Instead of offering her a model welcome complete with flowers and a liberating hug? They'd left the computer screen and arrived in the Vallejo bus terminal. His eyes looked her up and down insolently. Again, she wondered if it was Roberto trying to compare the face he was enjoying looking at now with the one made of megapixels. He was shorter than she'd imagined. Stocky. The head seemed to belong to a different body, a different neck. Her name appeared on his mouth: Ileana. Relieved, she smiled, and he walked over to her. There were no flowers or hugs, but as soon as he saw it was her, he proclaimed:

Here are the cheeks I want to lick.

Redeemed, Ileana took aim at his mouth and kissed the lips from the screen and confirmed the importance of temperature.

Roberto, I escaped.

You escaped from the screen. You're just like the photo you sent me.

I sent mine before you sent me yours.

You were sure of your good looks, he said teasing her. I didn't know if you'd like me or not.

They started walking towards the exit. Ileana stopped him and turned him around to face her. They were the same height and had the same color hair.

It was your mouth that convinced me. And it's the same one you have on your face.

Perhaps you thought I'd send a fake picture?

It happens on the internet.

My car's in the parking deck. Don't you have any luggage?

I'm at my yoga class, she said, laughing.

You were. I doubt it lasts four hours.

Perhaps you're not planning to take me to a yoga class?

Ileana was groping for the verbal stimulation that was their familiar territory. But Roberto looked nervous.

You're not going to call the cops, right? Are you sure you're at least eighteen?

Are you backing out, or what? You told me to come.

So that you'd come, Roberto teased.

That's right, laughed Ileana, enjoying the sexual frankness she'd discovered with Roberto.

In the car? asked Ileana as she settled into the front seat of the Tsuru.

Roberto started up the car and answered, I prefer a hotel.

A hotel? Why not your house? I want to listen to music while you make love to me. The music you sent me.

Anything goes in a hotel. You won't be Ileana visiting my house and I won't be Roberto who lives there surrounded by things...

Well, what sort of things do you have there? Ileana interrupted him. Pornographic art? Stuffed animals?

I have taxidermied animals, he joked.

Liar.

I'm a hunter and I don't think you'd enjoy my zebras and lions looking at you while I eat you. It might give them ideas.

Ileana thrust her hand into her bag to fish out the ringing cell phone. She let it ring and glanced at the number.

Is it the cops? Roberto asked.

It's a good thing the battery's going to die soon, Ileana said without acknowledging his question. I've never felt so light, she said, gazing out at the avenue. Look, just like those cars flying by. No baggage, no obligations, with Roberto and a way forward.

A way forward? Roberto asked. More like a hotel.

It's the same thing.

Roberto took a little bottle out of the door panel and passed it to Ileana.

A little shot of rum never hurts.

Ileana removed the cap and took a sip. The smell of rum went well with her idea of lightness.

I thought you'd be a bit smaller, Roberto said to her after watching her taking a long sip.

Are you calling me fat?

I didn't say that. I prefer meat to bones.

I thought you were taller.

Do I look like a dwarf to you?

No, it's just that faces don't tell you anything about the body. They leave it all to the imagination.

Did you imagine my cock in you? Roberto inquired, taking a swig from the rum with one hand and then returning the bottle to Ileana.

I will feel it inside me, Ileana said confidently, her eyes half-closed.

Did you think about my cock while your husband was doing it to you?

Ileana looked at him, annoyed.

Why do you have to bring up my husband?

Because you have one.

But he wasn't invited to our chat.

But you fucked him afterwards, right?

I didn't come here to talk about him. I came to get rid of him.

Did you fuck him and think about me?

Roberto held out his hand, asking for his measure of rum.

Aren't we at the hotel yet? Ileana interrupted him, irritated.

Or didn't you fuck at all? How long's it been since you fucked?

Ileana took another swig off the bottle and aimed her hand at Roberto's groin. She grabbed it roughly and was surprised to discover the hardness of his member.

What do you care? You're the one who's going to fuck me now.

He came immediately, didn't he? He didn't even give you time to get your engine running.

And you? Ileana said to him, furious and stroking him hard. Are you going to come in the car or are you going to make it to the hotel?

Roberto pushed Ileana's head down hard.

Take it out, he ordered.

Here? she said looking up at the windows.

What do you think, you little hottie?

Ileana lowered the zipper of his pants, searched for Roberto's warm, thick member, and covered it with her lips, her tongue, her palate.

Roberto's voice reached Ileana through the noise of her tongue on his turgid penis.

You got a room?

Ileana tried to pull away and raise her head. She felt she was being watched. But Roberto grabbed her hair tight and pushed her down, suffocating her. Ileana felt the car start moving again and then stop.

Roberto pushed her away and sought her lips. He kissed her.

He adjusted his pants and walked around the car to open Ileana's door. He took her by the hand and pulled her inside the hotel room. He threw her onto the bed, and he told her she was beautiful, that it was an honor to be there with her.

Stunned, Ileana looked at the space around her. A small room, the television in a corner near the ceiling. Deep purple curtains the same color as the bedspread. On the bureau, a roll of toilet paper that was reflected in the mirror. An odor of humidity and cigarette smoke.

A short-stay motel, Roberto said by way of explanation.

I've never been in one.

Never? You mean you were a virgin when you married your first boyfriend?

Again, Ileana rummaged for the cell phone she heard ringing inside her bag. But instead, Roberto answered his.

Later, he said. I don't know.

You can't get away for even a day, he said to Ileana who was looking at him in astonishment.

Well I did. You don't have another date, do you?

I have a date with a girl, he said, going over and and embracing her. See, I write to her every day and I can't quit. Her words turn me on. I think about her naked in my bed.

Ileana looked at him, smiling.

I hope she's online right now.

Roberto turned his back to her and sat on the bed, leaning his spine against hers and, pretending to type on the keyboard, he said out loud:

Gazelle?

Taurus? she answered, playing along with their screen names.

Look at yourself in the mirror, Gazelle, look how beautiful your cheeks are.

You make them beautiful.

No one's ever done that to you before?

No one. I want you to touch them with your tongue.

I touch them with my tongue. Lick your fingers and touch your cheeks with them.

Ileana did as Roberto directed her while she gazed at herself in the mirror.

Now I want you to take off your t-shirt. What are your breasts and waist like?

Ileana took her blouse off and tossed it onto the bureau.

Like a stone sculpture. Strong. My breasts are close together and they make a line, Ileana answered, staring at her own waist and her dark bra.

Brush your hand across your cleavage and now stick your finger in between your breasts.

I'm doing it, Ileana confirmed.

Now feel for your right nipple and touch it with your wet finger. Do you like that?

I love it, Ileana answered looking at her swollen nipple pushing up through the bra.

Take off your bra.

Ileana unhooked it as if Roberto's back weren't there, pressing against hers.

What are your nipples like?

Purple and big.

And are they erect?

They're like wooden spikes.

Just like my penis. My penis is a wooden spike that wants to thrust against your nipples like a sword.

Delighted, Ileana rubbed her breasts, squeezed her nipples until they hurt and began to breathe harder.

Without Roberto telling her, she unbuttoned her pants and stuck her hand beneath her underwear. She dipped her finger into her slippery vagina. The mirror reflected back the image of her contorted face, lost in the throbbing of her clitoris.

Roberto, make love to me.

Roberto watched her in the mirror while she touched herself. He undressed while Ileana kept her eyes glued to the mirror. Then he pushed her over onto the bed and penetrated her violently, eagerly. He squashed her, he touched her, he turned her over and exchanged words for thrusting and sucking, gasps and a racing heart, for moans and then the final explosion.

Undone, Ileana lay on the purple bedspread. Stretched out. Stunned with pleasure. Her telephone rang, but Ileana ignored it. Roberto's phone rang and he reached for it clumsily.

Later, I already told you. Yeah, yeah, the meeting.

Ileana emerged from her stupor and clung to Roberto's body, curling up against him.

Later? You're going to be making love to me later.

Yes, said Roberto, stroking her hair. Your jet-black hair. That's how the cops will be looking for you. Missing woman. Has jet-black hair, well-defined cheekbones, voluptuous hips and breasts.

Are you going to make love to me again?

Later, Roberto answered her. When I get back.

When you get back?

I'm going home and coming back in the morning.

Let's both go. Then I'll be able to see your animals without them eating me, Ileana said, her voice husky and her face buried between the pillow and Roberto's shoulder.

It's impossible, Ileana. I'm married, too.

Ileana opened her eyes.

Married? You never told me that.

I didn't think it was necessary.

But I told you from the very start.

I didn't think we'd ever see each other. It upset me to talk about my wife. What's more, I have nothing bad to say about her. She's a good person.

Ileana flipped over abruptly, turning her back to Roberto. He sat up and took her face in his hands.

It was a game.

A game that excludes good people.

Roberto tried to kiss her face.

We were playing at truth, Ileana declared.

The truth of our desire for each other, Roberto answered, running his hand across her breasts.

I escaped, Roberto.

You escaped on the screen every day, just like me.

You told me to come.

It was harder for us to see each other in your city.

You tricked me. And I got away for real.

I didn't force you to.

And how did you imagine I could come here without leaving for good? Ileana removed the hand that was softly stroking her waist.

I thought you'd make something up, but nothing permanent.

Roberto looked at his watch, stood up and began to dress.

I'll be back later.

You're leaving me in a short-stay motel.

I'll be back later. We'll have a good time and then I'll take you back to the bus station. You can tell them whatever you want at home.

Roberto tried to find her lips to kiss her but failed.

I'll bring you something for breakfast, he said before leaving the room.

Ileana no longer answered him. Dwarf, she muttered. She covered her naked torso with the purple bedspread and stayed there contemplating the bare walls. She heard Roberto's car start up and later the panting bodies in the next room. Someone flushed a toilet. She took a pack of cigarettes out of her bag and couldn't find a lighter. She found a pack of matches in the room. It was the same color as the curtains. She read the name of the hotel: The House of Enchantment. She looked at herself in the mirror, disheveled and alone, smoking in that strange room. Her cell phone rang, and she recognized the number on the screen and threw her bag across the room. Then she remembered that the battery was almost dead and retrieved it, anxious. She dialed.

Joaquín, they kidnapped me. I'll explain everything later. I'm in Mexico City. Write this down: House of Enchantment. Presa Atoyac Street, number 29. Come as quick as you can.

Ileana checked the time on her watch. It was three in the morning. She smiled and settled in to wait for breakfast.

Thursdays

I shouldn't have done it. But I couldn't help it. For me, all it took was to see them walk in with that excited yet guarded stride, she with her voluptuous figure and long, shapely legs and he, tall and slender, his gaze shielded behind dark glasses and his arm firmly wrapped around her waist. I caught sight of them from behind the half-open door of another room as they passed through the dark hallway, and, after they slipped by, I felt relieved that they were the same ones as always. The ones from Thursdays at five o'clock, the ones from Room 39. The weekly routine comforted me. In the whirlwind of hook-ups I saw every afternoon, that stitching together of Thursday after Thursday with love and desire was the essence of continuity. Who could be like them and steal away for a few hours in the afternoon, sometimes for just one hour, to find real sweetness in someone else's arms? Who might be able to forget all about Chino, Nachito and Lola, and the smell of beans simmering and instead, with their legs sheathed in silky stockings, permit themselves a lingering touch on a calf or a thigh with the exquisite attention of someone measuring and investigating the world of forms? Who could be the object of such mutual and consummated desire?

I never used to think like this, nor did I even really see my own legs. They were just good for getting me around. I hadn't grasped how undesired I was while I was witnessing the endless series of casual couples that wandered through these hallways, their moans muffled behind closed doors. But now I understood that just having a husband was no solace. Because if it were, why would the couple from Room 39 always return to reenact their inevitable coupling? Why would they come here once a week if they had some other option? Why the dark glasses? Why that specific time of day? Why were they in such a hurry?

At seven o'clock in the evening, the door to Room 39 opened. He glanced down the hallway and let the woman know the coast was clear. I returned to observe them, this time from behind, as they held hands in a lingering goodbye to prolong the rendezvous. I was making it last, too, and I'd dare to come a bit closer to the stairwell so I could watch their heads descend to the first-floor hallway that opened out onto the street. I hurried back to their room. I didn't want Teresa to beat me to it, because she did her rounds at the same time of day on the same floor. I would close the door behind me and take a look around at the mess, the same mess that in other rooms inspired weariness in me, sometimes even disgust. But there, I would fling myself face down on the bed and breath in all the aromas trapped in the used sheets. I extracted the smell of her perfume, like fresh-cut grass, and his woodsy aftershave.

I breathed in the sweat that dampened those over-laundered scraps of cloth and I'd find the traces of semen that escaped from the woman's filled, satiated vagina. Lying on that used sheet, my heart would beat wildly, and a rush of blood sent me into ecstasies. There, amid the evidence, I took part in the love ritual.

After a while, I would emerge into the shadowy hallway and deposit the bundle of sheets with more delicacy than usual into the basket overlfowing with linens. I was deeply grateful for these weekly visits, and I opposed any change of work schedule or floor. Those months had turned into a succession of pleasurable Thursdays. That's why I dared. When I first took the job, my boss emphasized the importance of discretion and never having contact with the clients. Avoid being seen, never speak to them. But I wanted to do something to show them how happy I was they were there, like at a wedding when you hug the newlyweds with all your heart. That's when I had the idea of the flower. The other maids teased me that a beau had given it to me. Nacho was so romantic, they joked.

It was a coral pink rosebud, just about to fully open. At four-thirty, the room was vacated by the previous clients, and I rushed in to clean it, planning not to leave until just before the hour. I didn't want to risk some other couple occupying that room, although I knew Tomás at the front desk already had instructions to make sure it was free every Thursday at five. I filled a glass with water, put the rose in it, and placed it on the scratched-up dresser. The rose was reflected in the mirror, and the bare walls and mattress marked with cigarette burns became tinted with the blushing color of the blossom. I breathed in the perfume of the flower that would celebrate the event this time, mingling its scent with the vapors and secretions of the lovers' bodies. I left at one minute to five, excited and also a bit nervous about the invasion that impinged on the couple's well-guarded anonymity. I put my trust in God, who, after all, had placed them in my path. During their two hours of lovemaking, my heart was all aflutter. I made beds, replaced toilet paper, and put clean towels in the other bathrooms, swept and walked around. And all the while, the image of the fresh, pink rose witnessing their naked bodies and their total surrender to each other stayed with me as if it were my feet in that glass of water.

I heard the sound of the door opening, and I peeked out from another room. I noticed that his gaze studied the hallway with greater caution. I took a deep breath and suppressed the temptation to run over and introduce myself, to confess that I was the rose-lady and that I hoped that I hadn't bothered them. I clenched my fists, not daring to watch as they disappeared at the bottom of the stairs. I went into the room. The same offering of disarray. Beneath the glass, now without the flower, was a fifty-peso bill. It was a kind of answer. I took it. After basking in the familiar aromas and the ritual to which I had added my rose, I walked out excitedly with the bundle clasped to my chest, only to then leave it regretfully in the pile of other stained sheets.

The following Thursday, five-thirty came and the people from Room 39 didn't show up. Still hopeful, I guessed there had been some slight mishap. But the next Thursday confirmed that the routine had been broken. Even so, I clung to the possibility that there had been a schedule change, a shift of location. Maybe she had a husband who had found her out or he had a wife who had gotten in the way. Maybe someone was sick, maybe someone had died. Maybe.

Ever since then, used sheets are a torture and a penance for me. And the smell of roses makes me sick. ⌘

What's There to Come Back to?

When a woman leaves home, you shouldn't let her back in. But how was I supposed to ignore her when she was out there all night? She knocked, and I said, *Who's there?* I told her, *Go away.* She didn't say anything. I heard her wool coat rub against the wooden door as she slid down to a sitting position on the step. I imagined her hugging the suitcase she'd left with, that big weekend bag, the one we used on those very rare occasions when it occurred to us to get out of the city. I threw eggs into the frying pan, and the sizzling oil drowned out the sound of her blowing her nose. It was November, and at this altitude it's always cold at night, and she gets all stuffed up from it. I took the eggs out of the pan and put them on a plate with a slice of ham—the last slice. Since she left, I buy very little. I never did the shopping before, and at first, I'd order a half kilo, but after a week, when I had to throw out most of the cold cuts because they'd gone all slimy and green, I realized that a hundred grams was enough. I started to enjoy going to the supermarket. It was clean and well-lit. At home, I only turned on the lights in the TV room and the bedroom. I no longer turned on the little lantern at the front door where Marta was now huddled in the shadows.

I attacked the yolks with a piece of bread, and then gazed deeply into the yellow magma as it slid into the coagulated whites. It annoyed me to hear her breathing out there. We never should have bought this house with its cheap materials. You can hear everything. When we moved here, we could even hear the neighbors flush the toilet, and with our last unmarried kid still living with us, we would all play at guessing who had done it. Marta would laugh. Back then, with Julian at home, she used to laugh a lot. He spoiled her, and she did the same to him. Girls. It would have been easier if we'd had a girl to spoil *me*. I always suspected that the son-of-a-bitch she left me for was just like Julian: cheerful, affectionate. But flattery and the lingering embrace are not my cup of tea. For me, a penetrating look is enough, like when I said goodbye to Marta as she was taking her brown coat.

"You're not going to stop me?" she asked, hurt.

"You want to leave. There's nothing to be done about it."

"Maybe you think that it's paradise living here with you?"

"It's just here, with me."

Why was she there now on the other side of the door? Three months of separation weren't enough to mend my soul. The pain kept bubbling up in me like the yolks that I wolfed down as if to eradicate the inevitability of her return with my jaws.

If she's a bitch, let her sleep like a bitch, I thought, finishing off the beer I drank every night to get to sleep. It's hard not to indulge in melodrama and to accept how difficult it is to sleep without Marta's body next to me every night, without her smell of creams and dried-up woman. I felt a shameless desire to say goodnight to her as I shuffled upstairs in my slippered feet.

Didn't she leave for love? Didn't she have the integrity to wound me with the truth? *You need a guy to be with, right? You're good for nothing by yourself.* I wasn't good for anything by myself, either. That's what I resented. I hated her for being gone, I hated her for humiliating herself right there behind the door, and I hated her for wanting to come back to me. She had betrayed me. No, not when she left. Even in my pain, I admired her openness to change, her attitude of every man for himself. Maybe life could've become more joyful. But she'd chosen this shared death again. Because habit protects and obliterates, and tacit understandings fill the silences. One becomes like a subscriber to life, saddled with a predetermined fate, unable to choose one thing over another.

The bed is cold, frozen, like beds always are when we mistreat them. But it's also wrinkled and full of crumbs, deprived of the kindnesses Marta used to bestow on the sheets that once awaited our peaceful slumber. It was enemy territory. Life has become enemy territory for me. At first, I was angry enough to think about finding her and duking it out with my rival. But it was she who'd left, and my punches weren't for the guy who'd offered her a transitory stop along the way. Maybe that's what love is, train platforms on a long journey. There are people who never leave the station. They're always missing something in their suitcases. Marta had gone off so sad that she'd forgotten her suitcase altogether. Not triumphant but broken. She couldn't get angry with me, she never could, even when I greeted her chatter about the book club or jazz class with silence.

What's there to come back to? Did she reassess? Did the hunk turn out to be not so hunky after all? Does he have bad breath? Is he grumpy in the morning? She's come back to grow old with me. To contend with being sixty, with the silence, the postscript after thirty-five years of marriage. I hate her. May she die of cold. May she sniffle and blow all night long, and may the snot turn into stalactites on her sore, red nose.

Fried eggs again for breakfast, the TV news. I think she's gone. Maybe she froze to death. Maybe we both froze to death. Marta always shouted: *A sweater, Victor, don't forget to take a sweater!* I wasn't a child, but I put it on, reluctantly. Wives turn into mothers, husbands become children. Julian and I never got along. One day, he told me he was going to take his mother out to dinner. *You don't like to go out at night, Pop.*

They came back laughing, stinking of wine. I didn't speak to them the next day. *You have bad breath*, I told them. No doubt, there behind the door, Marta would have that sour, up-all-night breath. The yellow lava once again flowed out onto the egg white, and I trapped it with a piece of stale bread. Then I heard her move. She heard my slippers brushing against the floor and dared to call out to me.

Victor, please.

There are bitches that live indoors, too, I thought, and I opened the door she was leaning against. She lost her balance and fell backwards onto the floor. Without looking at her, I returned to the table. *Thank you, Victor*, she said, as she patted her hair back into place. Clutching her bag and hugging her coat around her, she stood there, shaking off the night's chill. *I don't know how to be without you.*

Her first steps were uncertain. She asked permission to make herself some breakfast, to shower, to watch TV with me, to call Julian. The circles under her eyes, the fear, and the meekness slowly began to disappear, until she became the lady of the house again, just like always. Nothing changed. It was just that, occasionally, when I'd look at her flabby arms sticking out of her flowered blouse, I'd imagine them wrapped around another body, and then I hated her. I'd hear her laugh at something on the TV, and her happiness reminded me of the bed that had been wrinkled for three months, and her laughter that had been somewhere else. How she must have laughed it up! We never talked about our relationship. Silence as habit, and habit, in silence, finally put all the pieces back in their places again.

We rarely looked at each other directly, and we didn't make love anymore. Marta didn't dare to call a halt to my punishment of her, and I didn't want to stir up hard feelings. One morning at breakfast, staring at the sunny egg yolk on my plate, Marta reached out her hand lovingly and touched my forearm. *I need your caresses, Victor.* That was all it took. I gripped my fork and speared the hand that had touched me, pinning it to the table.

Now the silence is complete. She strokes her damaged hand when we have breakfast, when we watch TV, when we sleep, and when she absently gazes at the door that I once opened to her.

Ladies Bar

To Jorge

IF HER PARENTS SAW HER, THEY'D BE SHOCKED. She is, to avoid using the word respectable, a *good* girl. Accustomed to going to elegant venues where a certain class of people gathers. She has a taste for niceties, like men who stand up when she comes to the table and compliment her on her tasteful, discreet wristwatch. Like when the man she's out with orders the most expensive items on the menu for both of them and then asks for her approval. She's not the kind of girl who would know anything about short-stay hotels or cheap bars, at least that's what her parents think. From them, she hides that time she visited one of those garage-motels that have curtains to hide your car from view and that reek of the acrid odor of disinfectant, making the sex both impulsive and furtive for everybody.

Today she walks with Eduardo into the Florida bar, on a corner of the city's downtown. They've already visited a museum and walked along certain recently restored streets with buildings that have distinctive facades, which reveal an older city of canals and commerce. They've visited the historic La Merced convent and gone into ecstasies over its carved columns and majestic private cloister. It's not as if the place were normally open to the public, but the security guard, sensitive to the wishes of the strolling couple, allowed them to enter in exchange for a spontaneous, voluntary contribution. Smart of him, because after catching a glimpse of that lacey stonework and unexpected seclusion just a few feet from Roldán Street with its vendors' heaps of purple, brown, and yellow fried chilis, they don't hesitate to demonstrate their gratitude for the privilege and consideration. Were it open to the public, they wouldn't have had the pleasure of being the only people walking through the convent where, as Eduardo read somewhere, the famous painter Dr. Atl lived for a while. No doubt it was in the same state of neglect back then, too.

This simple walk has excited them as if they were setting foot in some forbidden city. Their city's forbidden city, like discovering a secret pleasure point on the body of someone you've lived with for a long time. That's why her ears perked up when they walked past the Florida, and Eduardo told her that when he was a teenager, he used to gaze at that bar and its plain entrance, which betrayed nothing of what went on inside. Back then as now, it had a sign that caught his eye: Ladies Bar. From where he stood on the sidewalk across the street, he told her, he used to imagine the women, their sinuous bodies, slender waists, low-cut tops, lacquered nails, and full lips. Sloe-eyed women, sated with pleasure, women with curvaceous figures and swaying hips. Fascinated, Mayra listened to him. This was an Eduardo she didn't know. Eduardo said that at sixteen he couldn't go in and he had no one to share his fantasies with. His mother's job was not far from there, and when he went to pick her up after work, he allowed himself extra time to stand there looking in from the outside. A man in a suit walked out straightening his tie. Another one emerged, stumbling drunk. But he never saw a woman hanging on anyone's arm. The women who, in Eduardo's imagination, would look like Catherine Deneuve in *Belle de Jour*. Elegant yet seductive. Demure yet stunning. Ah! Eduardo savored the memory as if he hadn't left that sixteen-year-old boy too far behind. And Mayra observed him, trying to find a way into that desire that had captured him back then. She wanted to accompany him to the heart of his fantasies, to the stimulation of that sign, Ladies Bar. She imagined him at night, eagerly stroking his sex, dedicating his orgasms to unattainable women. The mental picture of that horny young man turned her on.

Come on, she said, dragging him towards the Florida. Nothing's stopping you now!

Eduardo looked up and down the street. The afternoon shadows were lengthening, and it was true: except for his feeling that it was no place for Mayra, there was no one to stop him now. But what about you? *¿Pero tú?* He tried to object. I want to get a look at those women myself, Mayra insisted as they charged across the threshold that opened onto a small room with a dull-looking bar in the back and an old jukebox opposite a tiny dance floor. At first, Mayra was disappointed. She felt as if she were in a small town. It was an ordinary bar where any thought of adventure was inconceivable. It had nothing of that mysterious aura Eduardo had fantasized about. They sat down at the first table they found, near both the dance floor and the street, close to the jukebox.

And that's when they saw them.

They didn't have their hair in tall up-dos, and they weren't wearing dangly earrings, lots of eyeliner, or lip gloss. They weren't wasp-waisted or big-hipped. But they wore tight mini-skirts that emphasized sturdy, inviting legs, strong shafts that promised a moist paradise just above the hem. Mayra looked at them to her heart's content because in such a place it was permissible to stare. They're *ficheras*, Eduardo told her. B-girls. Mayra mentally reviewed the Mexican movies where she had first learned about the profession, and she was sorry these women didn't measure up to those tough, slum-dwelling types. She decided the place was short on squalor.

A man in the corner buried his face in the shoulder of a girl who allowed his other hand to move back and forth along her legs in a way that was at once insolent and reverent. Mayra gazed at those fingers offering their undesired performance, astonished at the lack of inhibition. Eduardo ordered two vodkas from the waiter. Beer would have been better, as Mayra had learned when she went to venues where the alcohol was of unknown provenance, but her excitement didn't leave room for caution. She took the vodka and drank because, with so many naked legs swirling around, she needed something to regain her composure.

Cheers, said Eduardo. Don't tell your parents. He treated her like a little girl, though she was almost thirty.

Don't tell your son, either, she said, mocking him. Eduardo was older and had a child from his previous marriage.

Here's to your sweet legs, he said.

Eduardo became hypnotized by the hem of a short girl's skirt. She was dancing near him with a man who was leading her around the floor with a certain panache, more to show off his own skill than out of desire for his partner. Mayra saw Eduardo's gaze lick the contours of those thighs. She saw him scan the woman's waist all the way up to her neck, where her long, dark hair fell, obscuring the outline of her cleavage. She didn't know whether it was their proximity to the little dance floor that made them feel obligated to watch those super-tight skirts and the legs that emerged from them as if the skirt were a formality, a mere loincloth over the dark sex that was sweating just beneath as the couple danced.

They're not like you imagined, are they? she asked Eduardo.

No, he answered curtly, taking another sip of his vodka and peeking out from behind the cold, wet windowpane of his glass.

Mayra imagined the *fichera* and her sturdy legs settling down onto Eduardo's lap. She imagined Eduardo's sex becoming aroused by the friction of those thighs and that come-hither hemline. How would she, Mayra, look in a skirt as short and tight as that? Just imagining the feeling of that close-fitting article of clothing excited her. No doubt she would attract some looks from the men. Surely Eduardo's hand would explore between Mayra's legs. There would be men who got hard just looking at her and her skirt.

Maybe you'd like a lap dance? Mayra teased him. She knew Eduardo wouldn't do anything so daring because she, the good girl, was here under his protection, because, she guessed, enjoying himself by getting it on with another woman was the very last thing Eduardo would allow himself. The *fichera* sensed the couple's attention and pressed herself even closer to her partner, who spun her around like a top. He bent their two bodies over so that they were practically touching the table, so that Eduardo could get a really good look at her luscious dark legs, so that Mayra might see Eduardo licking his own lips because he couldn't lick the other woman's skin. Mayra wanted to be the girl in the skirt.

Someone must have sensed her wish, because it wasn't the man sitting at the corner table who was stroking the short *fichera*'s legs, nor the one dancing with two middle-aged ladies, who came to this place to assuage their loneliness by dancing. It was instead the waiter, that funny guy who had already come over to inquire if the couple wanted to dance and who now returned to ask, would the gentleman mind if he had this dance with the lady? A dancing waiter, a harmless flunky whose job was to get the party going, who, as soon as Mayra set foot on the dance floor, overstepped his role of delivering drinks and collecting tips, making her spin and twist, taking her by the waist and steering her around with an obscene confidence that at first annoyed Mayra, a feeling she then forgot because when she looked over to seek Eduardo's approval, his eyes smiled back at her. The *ficheras*, with their sturdy legs and mini-skirts, formed a circle around her, the best and most demonstrative one getting very close. Yeah, that's how you do it! And Mayra raised her arms and shook her body as if the wild rhythm had seeped into her pores. Mayra closing her eyes and opening them in the midst of the shouts of Yeah, baby! Do it! And the gyrations of those excited women, accomplices to this debauchery stolen from passing pedestrians amidst the squalor, as much in another world on the other side of the door as Eduardo had been at sixteen. And then Mayra walked right into Eduardo's fantasies. Set upon by the men and women that surrounded her, by the women who grabbed her by the waist and then released her, by the men who were tugging on her arms and making her body spin like a top, by those bodies aflame with pleasure and impudence, she felt herself become all the women who had transported Eduardo into ecstasies when he was sixteen, those women with their lace panties, musky perfumes, artful coquetry, and soft, plum-colored lips. Mayra was all the women Eduardo could once only dream of out there on his island-sidewalk across Revillagigedo Street as he waited for his mother to leave work. Mayra now achieved the status of the unattainable woman thanks to the lewd ways of these impetuous men and women. She watched the girl who had danced next to their table approach her like a charging bull, and she realized she desired her as much as Eduardo did. And that here, amidst these volcanic spirits, she became both man and woman. Both desired and desiring. She wanted to touch beneath that skirt, to explore the viscous moisture the woman was offering to her, to Eduardo, to the man dancing with Mayra, to the man who now put a slow song by José José on the jukebox to dampen the fire, to apply a bolero like *Gavilán o Paloma* to the scene, to put the brakes on Mayra's soaring flight.

And when she caught her breath again and adjusted her dress that now was twisted and revealing more cleavage than usual, she looked for Eduardo at the table and suddenly became aware she had forgotten all about him. And a man came over to ask for the next dance, to take her by the waist and glue himself to her body where her sex was now throbbing for relief. The good girl tried to slip away, seeking Eduardo's protection, first at their now-empty table and then within the circle of dancers who had by then forgotten all about her. But the hand took hold of her and lead her off to a dark corner.

Don't worry, honey, he said. We come here to leave everything behind.

Señora Lara

SEÑORA LARA NO LONGER TOOK PLEASURE IN HER VIEW. The branches of the tree in her neighbor's yard had grown so thick that they blocked the daylight and cast her living room into shadow. That was where she liked to sit during the afternoons. Although she'd been living alone for three years, she took good care of herself, gathering her hair up on her head in a way that emphasized her neck and putting on a touch of makeup, just enough to feel good about herself. She'd been a handsome woman in a comfortable marriage until Jaime lost his mind and left her for a younger woman, almost the age of their own daughter. She stayed in the two-floor house with the balcony from which she could enjoy the view of all her neighbors' yards. The living room and her bedroom were in the back of the house overlooking the Aguirre's garden.

If there was one thing that upset Señora Lara, it was the afternoon gloom she felt when she'd sit down with her coffee and toast, a book in her hands. At first, it wasn't clear to her what was eclipsing her mood. It had something to do with the ongoing growth of a branch. When spring came, it became plain to see that it was indeed the brown branch covered with tender, green leaves that was taking up so much space. It practically split the window in two and now the light barely filtered through its palmate leaves. It's not as if I don't like trees, Señora Lara said, excusing herself. When she identified the reason for the darkness in the living room, she shared her observation with Celia, the woman who'd been her cleaning lady for a good many years. Over the next few afternoons she couldn't stop thinking about it. There was only one solution: to speak with the Aguirre family. Speak with them? Would they even open the door to her or let her into their home? Señor Aguirre was a politician, and there were always men in dark suits and a black car in front of their house, which was just around the corner. She didn't feel like ringing the doorbell just to get a *no*. She wasn't begging, she was just asking in a friendly way for them to share her concern. And for that to happen, it would be indispensable for them to see firsthand the view from her house, for them to understand how it might be that a beautiful branch covered in leaves was upsetting to her. She would write them a letter asking them to cut the branch and to come to her house and sit in her living room themselves—she'd invite them to coffee—so that they might understand what she was talking about. They, who owned such a tall and leafy tree, one that brought a hint of green to their home, shouldn't imagine that mutilating it gave her any pleasure. But the sunlight was her joy, her warmth. She'd lived for some years in southern Spain, and she loved the whiteness of everything there.

Back in Andalucía, she'd been happy. Newly married, drinking wine with Jaime in the afternoons after he came home from his hotel manager job. She used to paint on their little balcony that overlooked the alleys and the other balconies, and she'd taken such delight in the whiteness of the houses, the whiteness of the women's shoes and their smiles, the whiteness of the sheets where she and Jaime lay spooning, holding each other on weekend mornings and making love. She wouldn't speak to the Aguirres about the whiteness of things in her letter, nor about how in those days she'd luxuriated in the proximity of Jaime's body to her own toned body, aching with desire. She didn't care for melancholy because it made her vulnerable, and she was sick of feeling sad. You can only bear a certain amount of sorrow and then after a while you accept reality and milk whatever goodness you can out of it. There's always something good to be found. Even in milking, whiteness prevailed.

She went over to the secretary desk she and Jaime had bought in an antique store and took out a piece of paper. It was fortunate she still had some, since she no longer counted writing among her habits. If she wished to say something to her son or daughter, she called them. Her granddaughter was out of the country, and she'd only written a letter to her once. She was by no means sure what to write to a teenager to avoid boring her. When the girl didn't answer, she was sure she had annoyed her with her lack of interesting news. It was a good thing she wasn't writing to her now, because then she'd just ramble on about the branch and the dim light now filtering through the living room window where Miranda once crawled across the carpet when her parents left her in her *abuela*'s care. Her daughter had tried to comfort her, saying that young people didn't write letters anymore, that they used the computer instead. That's why now and then her daughter would read her the parts of the emails she received from Miranda that were meant for her *abuela*. By way of answering, at some point *abuela* had surprised her granddaughter with a phone call. She was a cheerful young woman. Her voice had light in it. Just like her own voice when she was young, when Jaime and David fell in love with her at the same time and the two of them sent her flowers, visited, and paid her lovely compliments. One day, the two young men ran into each other at the front door of the house, forcing her to make a decision. She chose Jaime, who was talkative and impetuous, and she bet the farm on his way of being. Passion has its price, and it's always unpredictable. Jaime couldn't stay still or remain in the same place for long. But he'd done it, staying by her side for thirty-five years. At a certain age, change may require somebody else's blood and determination to make you stop clinging to the furniture, the homes, the kids and grandkids, the certainty of death, and the unchanging view from your window.

Señora Lara wrote: Dear Señora and Señor Aguirre, I am your neighbor who lives on the other side of your garden wall, and it is in fact the tree growing along that dividing wall that is the reason for my letter. One of the branches has grown so much that it now blocks the daylight from coming into my room. Perhaps you will think I am exaggerating the problem, but I would be very grateful if you would accept an invitation to coffee in my living room on the afternoon of your choice so that you might better understand my concern. It is not some whim of mine, but lately this room in which I spend my afternoons gives me the feeling of being in a hole. I would be happy to welcome you at my home and to pay whatever gardening cost is involved in cutting the branch. Here is my telephone number, but please feel free to simply knock on my door. I am usually here. Thanking you for your kind attention, Señora Lara.

She read the draft several times, adding and subtracting words and feeling afraid that her request would make them think that she was a lonely, obsessive old woman. She knew that sort. There were always some around who complained about parties, open windows, and barking dogs. The ones that hated teenagers, people who laughed, and anything in life that was fancy-free and made noise. She'd had to deal with one of them with her own children, even with her own mother when their neighbor complained about the amount of time she'd lingered at the front door one night making out with her boyfriend. It wasn't Jaime then; it was her first boyfriend who kissed her and rubbed her breasts through her blouse, right there against the door, in the middle of the street, protected, or so they thought, by the darkness of the night.

When she was satisfied the letter was as friendly, clear, and convincing as it could be, she went personally to the Aguirres' door, which was flanked by the black car. She explained to the dark-suited men who she was and gave them the envelope. They wrote her name in a little book and made her sign it. She felt relieved that the delivery of the letter had been recorded. Her own misgivings about the chestnut tree's exuberant growth was also recorded in her request.

A week passed. There was no phone call, no knock at the door, no letter saying yes or no. Silence. She couldn't just sit there with her arms folded across her blue cashmere sweater, suffocating in that black hole. Coffee no longer tasted good to her. Her horizon had been reduced to such a degree that she was no longer comforted by the other houses' gardens, that unbroken continuity of the city's trees. So, she wrote a second letter in which she politely mentioned that perhaps they had overlooked her request—naturally, she was aware that they were very busy people, and she was sorry to bother them—perhaps thinking that hers was a small matter. But it was not, because her peace of mind depended on their attention to her request. It was only a branch, and it wasn't as if she wanted them to take down the whole tree; just that one piece of it, the one encroaching on her window. She tried not to sound pitiful, but she wanted to be sure they grasped the importance of this situation in her life.

The answer arrived on Friday afternoon. Señor Aguirre himself dropped by. Celia led the man in the gray suit into Señora Lara's living room. When he walked in, he apologized that Señora Aguirre couldn't be there because they had a dinner party that night and Señora Lara knew how long it took the ladies to get themselves ready. Señora Lara was surprised by the thoughtfulness of her neighbor to have come over to her house, and she told him so sincerely. Señor Aguirre was terribly sorry that she'd been obliged to send a second letter, but he was unaware that there had been a previous one until his wife mentioned it. I'm sorry, he said, underscoring his displeasure with the mistake.

I'm sorry to bother you, but kindly sit here so that you might understand my concern. Señora Lara stood up and gave Señor Aguirre her place on the cream-colored sofa.

Please, he said, moving to one side so that she might assume her original position. I think I can see from here.

Señora Lara had to sit down very close to the man's legs, and that flustered her. But from there she pointed out the branch to him.

You see, I love the light from the picture window. I read here. I spend a lot of time here. Now I feel as if I were in a hole.

It was that sentence, Señora Lara, that convinced me of the seriousness of your request, Señor Aguirre said with a genuine smile.

Señora Lara asked if he'd like a cup of coffee, but Señor Aguirre said that he'd prefer a whiskey, if it was all the same to her. Señora Lara said, yes, of course and went over to the sideboard where the glasses and bottles were kept. She asked Celia for some ice and poured the two drinks herself. Señor Aguirre was looking out the window when she returned. She didn't dare to slip in right next to him, so she sat down on the divan.

I thought you liked the view from over here, Señor Aguirre declared without moving. She went over and sat down next to him. She had not had a drink with a man since Jaime left.

They toasted, and Señor Aguirre said that he would personally see to it that the branch was cut.

Under one condition, he said before leaving. That I may come over to verify the improvement.

Please do, she said nervously, taking note of the elegance of her neighbor's suit once he stood up. You will like how the light comes in.

The next morning, Señora Lara heard the buzzing of the electric saw and observed with satisfaction how a man straddling one of the main branches was cutting the one that blocked her view, the impudent one. The severed limb bent down bit by bit until it fell to the ground with a dull thud. She rejoiced at the sound, the victorious trumpet blast that welcomed the light back in. She felt like sending a thank you note, but the condition Señor Aguirre had imposed made her wait.

Two weeks later, Señora Lara was embarrassed she hadn't sent her thank you note immediately. Now it was too late. How had she been so stupid as to take Señor Aguirre seriously? He was a politician, after all, accustomed to making nice with people and campaigning for votes.

On Friday, the doorbell rang, and Celia conducted Señor Aguirre into the living room. He was wearing a black sweater in which he looked more relaxed.

I'm sorry to have taken so long to come see your window, but I've been traveling, he said, excusing himself before sitting down.

You were very kind to have the branch cut so quickly. Look what a difference it makes! she said, gesturing at the window.

But Señor Aguirre didn't look towards the window. He gazed at her instead.

I can see you've gotten out of the hole, he said, smiling and he sat down in the same place as last time. He patted the sofa to indicate that he wanted Señora Lara to sit down next to him.

Whiskey? she asked.

And they sat facing the window until the sun went down. Señora Lara told him about her years in Andalucía, and he told her about his urban redevelopment projects. They had a second whiskey and laughed together until Señor Aguirre said he had to go and asked if he might visit her again the next day. He had liked the light, he said, and his wife was traveling outside the city. They were neighbors, after all.

His words caught her off guard. He'd had two whiskies with her because his wife wasn't home. People need company. That was all she could figure, the only reality that mattered to her.

Of course, she said, as she accompanied him on his way out the door. Of course, she thought, when she returned to her position on the sofa and looked out through the big window at the darkness. She imagined how the sunlight would come into her living room the next day. She took one last sip of whiskey and awaited the impending whiteness.

A Foreign Body

I'T'S NOT EASY TO GET RID OF A DEAD BODY, LET ALONE a dead body that belongs to someone else. Perhaps if I start at the beginning, you'll understand that I had run out of options. Then that business of my midnight run down the train platform will make more sense to you.

We were on our way to Zacatecas by train when we met her, when we met *them*, to be precise. Because that night at dinner in the dining car, there were four of us: my wife, Gonzalo, Silvia, and me. We were going to celebrate our wedding anniversary by visiting my wife's godparents and doing a little sightseeing. Gonzalo and Silvia were traveling from Mérida, and their relationship seemed to be in its honeymoon phase. In fact, we struck up a conversation when my wife and I were having a beer in the smoking car and in the unavoidable close quarters of those narrow wagons—anyone who's had the pleasure of traveling in a Pullman car knows what I'm talking about—I looked at Silvia's legs.

In those days, women wore stockings and knee-length pencil skirts. The informal jeans look wasn't yet customary for traveling. Gonzalo felt my visual invasion of their privacy, so he hastily placed his hand on the band of thigh between hem and knee to signal his ownership. In order to avoid any kind of bad feelings—and, now that I think about it, to keep Silvia in view, for who could've imagined what would later transpire—I asked what they were drinking and told the waiter to bring a round for everyone. Afternoon became evening, and we not only enjoyed some cocktails together, but we also shared a table in the dining car. Gonzalo was a businessman from Yucatán who was clearly older than Silvia, who herself was no more than thirty-five, with dark hair gathered up on her head that gave her an air of nonchalant elegance. Gonzalo was an amusing fellow, and my wife was being entertained by his anecdotes while I was enjoying the beauty of Silvia, who was quite aware of her own soft sensuality. We all bid each other goodnight, thinking that we'd surely still have a chance to share a coffee in the morning, and we retired to the sanctuary of our separate compartments. My wife said it seemed to her they weren't married. Perhaps they're recently married, I remarked, trying somehow to defend Silvia's honor. She's not wearing a ring, my wife stated in her characteristically perceptive way.

We hadn't yet arrived in Zacatecas when someone knocked on the door. We thought it would be the porter informing us of our arrival. But it was Silvia, with her hair down, literally right there in front of us at our sleeping compartment door wearing her dressing gown.

It's Gonzalo, she said, her voice breaking with emotion. He's not breathing.

My wife put on a jacket over her nightgown and followed her. I pulled on my pants and caught up to them. Wordlessly, we hurried through the next car. The only thing that impeded our haste was the metallic grind between cars as the train lurched from side to side. Fortunately, Gonzalo was in the lower bunk. A consideration of his age on Silvia's part, I assumed. He was very pale. I took his wrist as I'd seen done before in the movies. Silvia looked at him, weeping. My wife touched his forehead the way she would that of a child. Cold, ashen, no pulse. We called the porter while my wife held Silvia in her arms. I looked at Silvia against the arid landscape visible through the window, and she looked so vulnerable there in her navy-blue silk dressing gown. I imagined her engaged in the physical exertions of the previous night. I couldn't help but notice her cleavage and her hair in disarray. It profaned a dead man to ponder the cause.

We had to wait a while sitting there in the car. The housekeepers boarded to do the clean-up, and we'd already put the suitcases out in the hallway, including Gonzalo's. Silvia wept as she put his shoes on for him. None of us dared to cover him up with those narrow bunk-bed sheets. Someone arrived from the Civil Registry along with a doctor, and they signed the death certificate, which Silvia at first didn't want to take from them. Fortunately, all the paperwork was done on board the train because Silvia declared that she was his wife, so there was no need to inform anyone else while they were cremating Gonzalo, and she paid the bill with money she'd taken out of his pants pocket. We didn't have the heart to leave her all alone during these tedious formalities. My wife, who's a warm-hearted and caring person, asked her to stay with us in our hotel when we left the crematorium. Silvia calmly carried off the metal urn in which Gonzalo continued to be among us.

Was it something he ate at dinner? I asked awkwardly.

We had an argument afterward, Silvia bravely admitted and then began to sob. My wife rebuked my blunder with a look.

How about coming with us to our anniversary party tonight? I said to cheer her up.

My wife once again reproached me for my suggestion. Perhaps she'd prefer to go back to be with his people in Mérida, she said.

Silvia looked at me, seeking my protection. No, no, I can't go back to his people or my own. It became clear to us that no one knew that Gonzalo La Puente was traveling with someone nor that he'd died and become a pile of ashes in his lover's lap.

So, Silvia went to the dinner with us, and we introduced her as an old friend of my wife's, revealing to no one what had happened. Meanwhile, my brothers-in-law, cousins by marriage, and a lot of family members I didn't even know elbowed me in the ribs and hinted that I was a lucky devil to be escorting such a good-looking woman. Though you may justly condemn me for it, I felt like a lucky man at that moment. I looked at her legs and smiled to think that no one and nothing but my own gaze could have them. If I'd only known back then the far-reaching significance of what I then considered a stroke of good luck.

She was an agreeable woman, and my wife adopted her, feeling gratified by the act of charity to which her Catholic conscience gave its blessing. Together, the three of us made the return trip by train. I should say the four of us, because Gonzalo was travelling in Silvia's toilet bag along with her creams, perfumes, and hairspray. I figured that night had to be painful for someone who had begun the journey as a couple and now was returning with a man who'd turned into a bronze container. No doubt she would put him to bed in the lower bunk and lie down again in the upper as a way of assuaging the painful memory of that fatal journey. She must have been accustomed to the fleeting, to a relationship lived in pieces, in fragments, because that night my wife told me that Silvia had been Gonzalo's lover for eight years. He was, indeed, married. Someone would have to let Señora La Puente know, I said, unsure what was appropriate under such circumstances.

It's none of our business, my wife said.

And what will Silvia do? I asked, certain that the two of them had already talked it over.

She'll stay with us for a few days while she thinks it over and figures out what to do with Gonzalo.

My wife knew I wasn't going to get into any mischief, because if not she would've come up with some other solution. So, when we arrived in Buenavista, we took a taxi to the house, where we settled Silvia into our daughter Mariela's bedroom. She had no choice but to agree to the arrangement when she heard the story. One week later, Silvia had already switched her black outfits for lighter colors, and she began to accompany my wife to mass, to the supermarket, and to play cards. We found out she sang Yucatecan boleros and that she became a tad convivial when she drank a couple of Cuba Libres. The following Sunday, she even prepared a Yucatán-style suckling pig for us, slow-cooked *pibil*-style. I slept with great difficulty because of my irresistible urge to spy on her while she slept, to gaze at her body stretched out across the sheets. Mariela told her mother that she'd already spent the night on the study sofa for two weeks. When was the lady leaving? My wife told her that she simply couldn't kick her out of the house after such a terrible tragedy, and that our daughter was being a fusspot. The fact is that, in order to placate Mariela and even though it would be more expensive, we told the live-in maid we wanted her to just come during the day, and we converted the maid's room for Silvia. After that, no one dared to tell Silvia she had to switch rooms, not even Mariela herself, who watched her praying to the urn that now was on her dressing table right next to a fuzzy pink French poodle that Mariela's boyfriend Javier had given her. So, one morning when Silvia was at the beauty salon, our daughter went into her bedroom to retrieve her most beloved possessions and made a pleasant little nook for herself in the maid's former quarters.

After a month, my wife's charitable spirit began to wear thin. Go to La Villa cemetery and get a niche for that damned urn, she said with utter irreverence.

One afternoon, I knocked on Silvia's bedroom door. The two of us were alone together in the house because my wife no longer invited her along for shopping or to see her friends, and my daughter now avoided spending time in her new quarters with its view of the laundry room.

Silvia, I've found a niche for Gonzalo.

She looked at me, her eyes bright with tears, and turned towards her powdery lover.

I don't know if I can live without him. I know I'm a burden to all of you and you've been so kind to me. I'm going to leave soon. I'm waiting for a letter from my aunt in Campeche.

I was so distraught over her situation that I begged her not to worry about it. While I was speaking with her, I contemplated her trembling lips that transformed into a smile tinted the alluring flame-red she always wore.

But you're so beautiful! Soon you'll make a new life for yourself, I said, trying to lift her spirits. Then she kissed me on the cheek, the kiss of a naughty little girl.

Did you tell her about the urn? my wife asked me that night while we were strolling down the sidewalk after dinner. It was impossible now to speak privately inside the house.

She doesn't want to be separated from him, I said by way of reply. She gave me a sharp look. She knew it was my job to desecrate the charity that she herself had made such a point of offering. That night, Mariela asked me the same question before going to her room.

You've told her about the niche, right?

I couldn't sleep. I lay there staring at the darkened lightbulb hanging from the ceiling thinking about how I hadn't bought a fixture to cover it since we'd moved into that house fifteen years earlier. Suddenly, stirred by outrage, I arrived at a solution. So, I entered her bedroom, turning the doorknob cautiously, and I contemplated Silvia with her dark hair in disarray and the same nightgown peeking out of the neckline of the same navy-blue dressing gown she was wearing that night two months ago when she informed us of the terrible event. Her knees were exposed, and the smoothness of her feet inspired me to caress them. What am I saying, "caress" them! No, to slide my tongue between her toes. She moved a little, and then I remembered the reason, the mission that my role of father and head of household commanded me to accomplish. So, I took it from the dressing table, looking at my reflection in the mirror as I removed her lover from the intimacy of the alcove. Pardon me, I whispered to the dead man, and then I knelt in front of the feet on the bed to gaze again at the arches and pink ankles, to reach out my hand with the improper aspiration to caress them.

I left quickly without closing the door behind me.

The city was deserted, so it didn't take me long to get to the station and to run to the platform as if I were late for a train and to deposit him there on the steps of one of the cars on the train to Guadalajara. I came home in short order, but at the house they'd already discovered Gonzalo was missing. My wife had her arms around Silvia who was weeping on her bed, and when no one was looking, Mariela put her pink French poodle back on the dressing table.

You could have just told me to get out, Silvia blurted out between sobs. That's no way to treat a person. You, who have been so kind to me.

I couldn't bear it for one more second. I knelt down in front of her, at her glorious feet and knees, without any regard for my wife's presence or her belated compassion.

I had to take him to the station, I had to get rid of him. Don't you see, Silvia? Gonzalo made me sad. I also loved him in those few kilometers we knew each other. He was making everyone in this household sad. It was an act of love, to not condemn Gonzalo to the dark hole of a niche. We need you to be happy, Silvia.

And as my wife let go of those shoulders that she'd been holding with such maternal zeal, I looked at Silvia's feet and felt sure they were well worth a dead man.

The Perfect Woman

I USED TO WALK THROUGH THIS PARK WHEN I VISITED my mother. She didn't live far from me. I would dress up because one Thursday a month she and I went out to eat together. We'd made this arrangement after my three children were born and she became a widow. We had to carve out some space for ourselves. On those days, she wasn't a grandmother or widow, and I wasn't a wife or mother. We were just mother and daughter, an opportunity that the circumstances of our lives and my brothers and sisters had stolen from us. So, when I went out with her, I would wear stockings, a tailored skirt, and the pink sweater with the pearl neckline, and I carried my brown suede handbag. We'd choose a nice restaurant, and mother's hired car would drive us there.

You might think that kind of outfit isn't appropriate for walking across a park in this city, but I'm not some sort of shrinking violet. I didn't want to miss out on the pleasure of walking along lost in my own thoughts beneath the jacaranda and ash trees and looking at the masses of hydrangea which reminded me of my childhood home, the one where I used to live with my parents and brothers and sisters, the one they sold when things didn't work out with the butcher shop and we had to squeeze the whole family into an apartment in the Colonia Roma.

My mother hated that apartment, so she didn't even bother to put flowerpots on its poky little balcony. Nothing like her bougainvillea at the San Ángel house. She wilted for a while, and it turned out that it was hard for her to sprout new leaves, new foliage to shelter us kids with. Losing the garden was terrible for my brothers and sisters and me, too. But the street offered us a bit of greenery and a freedom that was new to us. It was easy for us to accept the sunshine on the rooftop as a substitute. We ran off every afternoon.

My mother doesn't live in that apartment anymore. If she did, you wouldn't find me here now. Thursdays was the day we ate together, the day my husband took care of the kids. He understood what a great idea it was. He took them to the club and helped them with their homework, and I would be off with mother, drinking wine and getting happy and a touch nostalgic, as we recounted our memories of breakfasts in the big house in the nook next to the dining room where we used to spend most of the day. That's how the weekends were, anyway, though Mom would say that's how it was all the time. Every single day, the morning slipping away from us as we sat there in our robes with our coffee and cigarettes. She would be overcome with a massive case of yearning for what she believed was once half our lives: that table and the conversations we had around it. Then she'd light up another cigarette. How my mother smokes! I didn't think I would pick up the habit. But look at me now. Do you have a cigarette?

One day I was walking along in my brown skirt and pink sweater with the matching handbag and the silky stockings that my mother kidded me about, and there he was sitting on the bench. I was a little taken aback because he was a grimy man with a filthy, sooty jacket and a face I didn't dare to look at. I held myself very tall and pretended he didn't bother me so I could get past the bench, like it was nothing. I held my purse close to my hip and picked up my pace. My high heels made it impossible to run, as did my certainty that I shouldn't let him see I was in a hurry. Showing fear makes a person more vulnerable. I know that's how it works with dogs. They attack you if they smell your fear. But naturally I felt his gaze going right through me. You know how it is. A woman knows that feeling. The burning eyes and you becoming transparent, naked. Not to mention a bit flattered, I have to say. I passed the bench and kept my gaze fixed on the hedge-lined path. But his thick voice called out to me.

Hey.

I couldn't keep going as if nothing had happened. There was something of an appeal and a command in those three letters. I looked at him without saying a word, asking with my eyes if he was speaking to me.

Ma'am.

Then I stopped.

Sit down, please.

I stood there frozen in front of the green bench. His hands were clutching the edge. I don't know why my attention was drawn to them. I guess it was easier than looking at his face.

Don't be afraid.

I looked at his face then because there was something courteous in that turn of phrase. He had a haggard, ashen face, and his high cheekbones rose out of a scruffy beard. He reminded me of my cousin Felipe. I don't know why I thought of my cousin Felipe who always used to play with my brothers and looked at me as if he wanted to say something that he never did. He was killed in an accident. That sort of thing happens to boys. I hope it doesn't happen to mine. But Felipe told me again to sit down and so I did, on the far end of the bench and I sought the protection of the metal armrest. I sat very tall and rigid, without leaning back and with my knees and feet pressed close together. I looked at my just-shined shoes with the raised geometrical shapes, the ones that revealed my instep.

Don't think I was born here.

I didn't say anything.

Because I didn't want him to think I was prejudiced against him, you know? I set my handbag on my lap and turned to look at him without moving my body, just my neck and my ears pretending politeness. My hands fiddled with the handle of my bag, twirling it around as I waited to find out what else the man wanted to say to me. But he stayed quiet and didn't even look my way.

She was perfect, he said in a low voice.

Do you live here? I answered. I was anxious to be on my way.

He pointed at the park maintenance shed.

They let me sleep there. I take care of their shears and barrels. Sometimes I wear their rubber boots when I want to splash around in the fountain, when it has water in it, because the dirty bitches don't wash it every day. They make out with the truck drivers and I see how they slide their hands under the men's overalls. This place here's a dirty world, but a little less dirty.

I got up, and he saw I was leaving.

Sorry. I shouldn't talk about that shit. She used to tell me that, too. When I wanted to pet her, she pushed my hand away and she called me dirty. You make me sick, she used to say. Sick, ma'am...miss...

He sounded desperate.

I sat down again.

I would disgust her now, but back then I didn't. I was a respectable man with a car. Do you have a car? She had a car. That's why I didn't know when she was going out. She left when I left, which is to say, every single day. She went to see him. She was so pretty all dressed up. Just like you, with the silky stockings and the elegant skirt. She didn't like pants. Or my bad breath, either.

And then he laughed like crazy.

He frightened me. I glanced at my watch. I was already running late.

Sorry, but…

Always on time! She was, too. She always had the house ship-shape, my clothes ready, the food perfectly prepared, her hair perfectly styled. People sang her praises when they came to the house. We didn't have kids and she told me it wasn't 'cause of her, it couldn't be 'cause of her. I don't know why she was so sure about that. But who could tell her otherwise when she did everything else so well? She even called my mother every day and she gave my dog Bull his bath. She had him perfectly groomed by the time I got home from the office. Accountant. Yes. Here are my accounts…

He took a little notebook out of his pocket.

Forty lilies, ten rose bushes, three palm trees.

He held his notebook out to me, smudged with dirty fingerprints. I saw his neat writing, his perfect numbers.

This is on the main path. Two dogs, a rat, five squirrels. It's full of squirrels. Two bitches. Also full of bitches.

Then he bent his head over his notebook and took a pencil stub out of the same pocket. He made a note: One pretty lady. Pretty ladies never pass by.

I wanted to leave, but his words just kept coming.

I have to…

Go. Yes, I know, go. Everyone has to go. Except me. Look, I live here and at night the park is mine. All mine. You hear a rat now and then in the garbage cans, but I close up the maintenance shed, or I go out along the paths to the fountains and I run. I run hard. A man my age better not get sick, and certainly not a man in my situation. They would be picking up a dirty corpse. I hope you'll pardon me. If I had known I was going to see you today, I would've bathed. I would've washed my clothes and then I would've put them back on damp, at dawn before the bitches that wash the fountain come and the guards that watch over the park and the people that run early and before the fat ladies who throw their mats on the ground and do what the teacher tells them to. Before, before. I know how to prepare myself for a woman.

He didn't frighten me, though perhaps you don't believe me when I say that. He made me feel peaceful. He was big. His hands were strong and full of knots. I felt like a little girl sitting next to him.

Did you play in the park as a child?

He asked me this using the familiar *tú* and looking directly into my eyes. Then he covered his mouth.

Sorry. My breath. It's been a long time since I spoke with a woman. Those other ones just come to get me excited. They sneak into the maintenance shed and try to fondle me. I'm not made of wood and I end up doing what they want me to when they pull down my overalls and get all horny. Face to face? No, honey, we don't want to smell your mouth. They laugh at me, the bitches.

Then he grabbed my hand.

I don't know what I'm saying, I don't know how to be with an elegant woman. I've forgotten how. She never let me say such things.

I left my hand resting there between his dirty ones. It looked so white and prim to me with its wedding ring, there between his blackened man-hands. I liked my clean hand with its lacquered nails.

She wore pearl earrings and had a ring like yours with my name on it, he said softly. Every married woman carries the name of a man on her finger.

And he felt for my ring with his fingers and slipped it off. I have no idea why I didn't put up a struggle. He tried to read the name engraved inside and raised it up to the daylight that was filtering through the ash tree in front of us.

They gave them to us like that, I said, excusing myself to him. We didn't notice it at first and then we just decided to leave the engraving for later.

You shouldn't leave anything for later.

I became alarmed.

No. I should go.

I took my hand away from him.

Are they waiting for you to eat? He was looking directly at me.

Yes. My ring... I was anxious. I figured this was some sort of trick I had fallen for like an idiot.

You don't think I'm going to keep it, do you? What would I do with it? Huh! It doesn't even have a name on it.

He tossed the ring into the grass on the other side of the path. I froze.

I won't be able to explain it, I said calmly.

Don't explain it. She didn't explain anything to me. She just left.

My mother's waiting for me, I said. I didn't want to hear about his past.

Do you know what? he said, looking at me again without paying the least attention to what I had said to him. You aren't like her. You're prettier. Listen to me: You're really the perfect woman.

His legs covered with those dirty pants were pressed up against mine, and he had taken my hand back. Cornered like that, any idea I had of getting up and walking away evaporated. It was as if my power had left me with the ring. I leaned back against the bench and, without speaking, we waited for the evening to come. When the park lights came on, he explained to me that they were smart lamps and that thanks to them he wasn't left in complete darkness, he could see. Even when there was no moon.

Do you like parks? He put his arm around my shoulders, and I didn't mind the greasy jacket on my pink sweater.

Yes, I answered, looking at what I thought was a cloud of hydrangeas.

It's not so bad living here, he said. And he stood up, reaching out his hand so I would come along with him. We started walking as night fell. I liked his stride. His open shoes with no laces next to my new, strappy shoes. We walked arm in arm without talking, and I was thinking about the garden at my old house and its hydrangeas and how happy my mother would be when I told her. After our walk, we went into the shed and he motioned towards the mattress. He said he would be right back and, when he returned, he had washed his hands and face. I saw Felipe's skin and Felipe's eyes. Maybe he would have been just like that if he had grown up to be a man. And just like my cousin, he didn't say a single word to me. He just held me. When he tried to caress me, he got frightened and took his hand away. But then I took it and placed it on my breast, right on top of the pink sweater.

It's amazing. You really can't make out the pink of my sweater anymore. They don't come around to bother him anymore. At night, we wash in the fountain, and he's beautiful when he's naked and clean. I became his woman, and sometimes during the day I feel the urge to talk with someone here on this bench. To tell you that my mother's waiting for me to go out to eat with her, and my children, too. But I like this park with its ash trees and hydrangeas and the night and the fountain. This is where I live. It's perfect.

Do you understand me? No, don't go. I won't steal anything from you.

The Caretaker

THAT VERY MORNING SHE'D THOUGHT TO HERSELF, I should write down my name and address on a piece of paper and put it in my purse to have some sort of identification. She always said she'd fill out the page marked Personal Information as soon as she broke out her new date book, but it was March already and she'd totally forgotten about it. Now, hanging onto the bus's handrail above her head, she looked without seeing at the laps of the passengers in front of her whose knees she brushed against occasionally. After two years of working the same office job, she was so used to the morning commute that she instinctively knew how to ride out the sudden stops, where to place her arm and plant her feet. She would've preferred to make the trip sitting down, mostly because she took the opportunity to give her lips a final touch-up and pat her fluffy, lacquered hair-do back into place. With the morning rush, it never stayed put like it did on the weekends.

She'd been traveling in a stupor, afflicted with a strange exhaustion that felt like a hangover after a sleepless night. That was strange, since on Sunday she and Germán had done what they always did: watch TV with her aunt, have the quesadillas that Meche sold on the corner for supper, and then, after their music program ended at ten o'clock, Germán said goodnight because he had to get to the garage by seven the next morning. A feeling of weakness was washing over her with increasing intensity, and, alarmed, she leaned forward so that the air from the open window would blow directly onto her face. She switched her purse to the other shoulder and changed the position of her feet, and again became lost in contemplation of the passengers' laps, her head resting in the crook of her elbow. A cold sweat suffused her body, and she couldn't utter a sound to ask for help.

No doubt she'd ended up right there on those very same thighs wrapped in different sorts of cloth, had taken a brazen nosedive right onto the laps of the startled passengers in her red dress and pointy high-heeled shoes, purse still dangling from her shoulder. Now, gazing at an unfamiliar ceiling, Marisela began to speculate. She had no shoes on. Her feet, still crammed into Lycra stockings, were touching a synthetic bedspread, and the texture made her shudder. She was groggy and afraid of finding out where she'd wound up. It wasn't a hospital: the bare lightbulb hanging from the pistachio-green ceiling, the smell of cooked beans, and the quilted bedspread beneath her made that clear. Slowly, she turned her head. Next to the bed was a Formica table, and her black purse hung from the backrest of the nearest chair. What assailant would've laid her down on a bed, taken off her shoes, and put her purse within reach?

The Caretaker

In the next room she saw a stove, but there were no sounds coming from over there. A pot on the burner was giving off the odor that permeated the apartment. On the back wall was a television on top of which sat a beige enamel vase holding two faded cloth roses. She let her eyes travel around the rest of the room. Near the foot of the bed was the entrance door, also painted pistachio green, on which hung a calendar. To one side of it was a wedding photograph in an oval frame. That sign of human life reassured her, and gradually she raised herself up to a sitting position on the bed.

The little red flowers on the bedspread made her dizzy, and she returned her gaze to the wall opposite the door, searching for windows. She saw two, high above a large wardrobe. She lowered her feet to the floor, and, reaching out to steady herself on the chair, she tried to stand. She crept over to the wardrobe and again felt the wooziness she had experienced on the bus. Quickly, she reached for a bottle of cologne that was on the wardrobe's built-in shelf. She opened it hurriedly and breathed in the aftershave's masculine scent. She caught sight of herself in the round mirror. She was pale, but her hairdo was still in place. Two other aftershave lotions, a deodorant, a condom, and a hairbrush were also reflected there in the mirror. All these things appeared to belong to a man and, intrigued now, she opened a drawer where undershorts, t-shirts, and socks coexisted all jumbled up together. She turned the key that was in the wardrobe door, and inside, the skirts of flowered pink dresses stood out, bright against blue and brown pants.

The alcohol in the aftershave had revived her, and she thought the time had come to leave. She'd write a thank-you note to the couple including her address, so that she might return their kindness someday. She sat in the chair where her purse hung and took out a pen and a sheet of paper ripped from her date book. She smiled, thinking of the ironic usefulness of it despite her failure to fill out the Personal Information page. She took the dusty vase from the TV and placed it on top of the note so that the occupants would see it there. She slipped her feet into her shoes, brushed her hand across the puffy bedspread to smooth it down, and, with her purse once again on her shoulder, she headed for the door. She turned the knob but couldn't open it. She looked for the deadbolt that had to be keeping it shut, but in vain. They had locked her in. She would have to wait until someone came back.

She put down her handbag and went to the kitchen to peek through any window that might give her an idea of where she was. As in the big room, there was a window like a small air vent high up. She dragged over a chair and climbed up to reach it, but it was impossible to see anything unless she stuck her face inside the vent's casement, and the chair wasn't high enough to allow that. She went back to the bedroom and climbed up on one of the wardrobe's shelves. She heard the racket of trucks and voices outside. But there was no other clue that might help her figure out on which street or in which neighborhood she now found herself.

Exhausted, she sat down on the bed. The effort had been too much in her still delicate state. She checked the time: it was noon. She should let her job, her aunt, or somebody know where she was. She squatted facing the front door. She could see a dark, empty hallway through the keyhole. She stayed there for a while, listening for footsteps, until she thought she heard something. She saw a woman's legs in stockings and high heels. She brought her mouth close to the keyhole and called out:

"Ma'am, here, ma'am!"

She watched the legs slow down and pause for a moment. She imagined the brain above those legs trying to figure out where the sound was coming from. She called out again, this time louder, but the woman continued on her way. Marisela gave up. She would wait. With luck, the worst they could do at work was dock her pay, and she'd get home at the same time as usual. She turned on the TV and stretched out on the old bed.

The sound of the opening door woke her up. It was night, and in the darkness, she couldn't make out who was coming in. The man turned on the light and apologized.

"Did I wake you up, beautiful?"

Marisela was left speechless by the way the stranger addressed her.

"You must be starving. I'll prepare some steaks and warm up some beans so we can eat."

The man spoke with feeling as he took off his sweater and hung it from a hook next to the door. He disappeared into the toilet that was behind an oilcloth curtain, and Marisela heard the strong flow of his urine, and then the flush whisking it away. Reappearing, he washed his hands at the sink that was outside the bathroom and casually approached the old bed where Marisela, having tugged her dress down over her legs, remained motionless. He sat on the edge of the mattress and took her face in his hands the way her father used to do.

"How lovely you look."

Marisela figured that she had been ruthlessly taken prisoner by this stranger, who was no doubt the apartment's only inhabitant. But the man caressed her hair with his thick hand. She couldn't keep her lips from trembling.

"I'll cover you up right away," he said.

He took a shawl from the wardrobe, threw it over her shoulders, and closed it in front for her as if she were a little girl. Then he went into the kitchen. Marisela tried to gather her wits about her, to regain her power of speech so that she could say thank you, and then leave. The man reappeared carrying two plates.

"Come, eat."

He turned on the TV and sat at the table. He ate without looking at her, engrossed in the black and white screen in front of him. Hungry, Marisela resisted the impulse to interrupt him, and she also ate. When he finished, he remained immersed in the TV. He had a wide, brown face and thick, black hair that was glossy from the tonic that he probably used every morning to slick it back. His arms were smooth and hairless, a wristwatch the only thing interrupting the dark luster of his skin. Uncomfortable with the silence, Marisela stood up and cleared the plates, which she washed in the kitchen sink. She gathered up the napkins and soda bottles. After she finished, she sat down in her chair, determined to speak.

"Would you kindly tell me where the bus stop is, and what line I should take to get home? It's late and they're waiting for me."

"Your home?"

"Yes. I'm very grateful for your help, but my aunt and boyfriend don't know where I am."

"You're already at home," he said.

"Thanks, that's very nice of you. I hope to return the favor one day and invite you to come to dinner at my aunt's house, because my parents live in Michoacán, you see, but all the same, when you come . . ."

The man didn't seem to be listening. He rose to his feet and took out a cot from behind the wardrobe.

"But there's no need," Marisela insisted, pleading.

The man unfolded the cot on the other side of the table, right next to the kitchen door, and took two blankets out of the wardrobe. Standing in the middle of the room, Marisela didn't know whether to cry or to start punching him in the chest. He gave her a blanket. Again, he took her face between his thumb and forefinger, and turned it towards himself.

"Rest now."

He turned off the light and went over to the cot. Standing speechless next to the table, Marisela watched as he took off his shirt, leaving his smooth, ample belly fully exposed. Intimidated, she lay down on the bed with its flowered quilt and covered herself with the blanket. She rested her head on the warm batting, but it only served to inflame her feelings of impotence and fury. She thought about her aunt, who would be out of her mind with worry, and Germán, who would have called around to all the hospitals and to her coworker Claudia. Nobody would know why she hadn't made it to the office that day, why she hadn't called in, why she hadn't come home. Between the noisy breathing of the man with whom she shared the room and the crashing waves of her unresolvable anxieties, she finally fell asleep.

The man woke up early. Marisela heard him stirring on the cot. As he made his way to the bathroom in the faint light from the small window lighting the room, she noticed something shiny hanging from his neck. He came out of the bathroom, his hair wet and his torso still naked. Marisela could make out that the bright object was a key. She slowly concluded that it must be the key to the front door, and that he would wear it beneath his shirt to work, or to wherever the hell he went, while she waited here with her sweaty, dirty red dress and the agony of eight more solitary hours. The man came out of the kitchen with two steaming mugs and approached Marisela.

"Here's your coffee, beautiful."

Marisela sat up, pulling the blanket up to her chest, and took the cup.

The two sipped in silence. He looked at her face, spellbound, and she buried her own gaze in the steam from the coffee.

"If you want to change, there are dresses in the wardrobe. It's been over a year, and the worthless bitch isn't gonna come back and give me shit about it."

He bent down and bestowed a kiss on Marisela, along with a strong smell of deodorant and cheap cologne. He took his sweater from the hook and closed the door behind himself. Marisela heard the key turn in the lock.

She had eight long hours to come up with a plan. She decided that there was no other way. So, when the man returned that evening, Marisela greeted him with a smile, wearing one of his wife's dresses, which featured a low neckline and, since it was a bit small on her, was rather tight around the hips. She'd put on lipstick and eye shadow, washed her underarms with soap, and combed her hair with his tonic. While he cooked, she found excuses to join him in the kitchen, which was so small that their bodies couldn't help but brush up against each other. He had a beer with dinner, but this time he found it hard to concentrate on the TV. While Marisela washed the dishes, he came to get another beer and stood behind her, transfixed by the sight of her hips.

Marisela brought him one more beer and told him she was sleepy. Standing next to the bed, she started to undress with deliberate languor. She watched him as he approached her, his gaze dark. She turned off the light and breathed deeply, summoning up her desire for freedom so that she might find a way to endure the kisses and the enormous body on top of her. She took off his shirt. He squeezed her buttocks and ran a hand between her legs. Marisela caressed the man's back, pressed her mouth against his hairless chest, and took the key between her lips, sliding the chain over his head and disdainfully tossing it to the floor. With his pants around his knees and her naked body beneath him, the man ejaculated quickly and copiously, falling to one side, breathing hard and unevenly.

Marisela waited for an hour, maybe two. The man's semen dried between her legs. Slowly, she rolled off the mattress, and, sliding the key along with one foot, she crept over to the bathroom, where she'd left her red dress and shoes at the ready. Hurriedly and silently, she got dressed, took her purse and the shawl, and made her way to the door, keeping an eye on the man who was sleeping with his pants down around his knees, sated. She inserted the key and turned it slowly, rotating the knob and opening the door. She looked back at him, still asleep. She closed the door behind her. Then the key fell, and she could hear the creaking of the mattress springs, but she was already out in the street in front of the old building and hurrying away.

It took a while for her to recover, to take in what had happened to her during those two days, to get over her own daring and the memory of the stink of the man's cologne and beer washing over her. She didn't tell the whole story to anyone, not exactly the way it happened. On Sunday, they ate Meche's delicious quesadillas, and Germán was holding her especially close. She needed him, and she let herself take shelter in his caresses and embraces. After her aunt said goodnight, she and Germán said goodbye with a long kiss.

Marisela put on her nightgown. She removed the bedspread from the bed, but somehow the quilted texture of it and the pattern of little red flowers made her dizzy. A voice from the window consoled her.

"I told you this was your home, beautiful."

Meaty Pleasures

THE SATURDAY VISIT TO THE BUTCHER SHOP WAS MANDATORY. Papá and Mamá got all excited when they started to think through the shopping list out loud at breakfast: a rib roast and a leg of lamb, a skirt steak and some lean ground beef, a bit of pork fillet. My sister and I would plunge our spoons into our cereal, rescuing those poor little flakes from the white surface, which was the antithesis of the bloody list they mercilessly narrated, spoiling our appetites. I want chicken, said Estela, just to be a pain in the neck. The two of them shot her a dirty look for her attack on their meaty catalog. They told us to hurry off and make our beds and brush our teeth, and then, resigned to our fate, we got into the car that would bear us off triumphantly to the butcher shop in Colonia del Valle.

Estela and I had found a newsstand on the corner and, since we had our allowances with us, as soon as we got out of the family rattletrap, we'd run off to choose two comic books each. We could've read them sitting right there on the bench, but we liked to make them last for the whole week, reading them stretched out on our bedroom rug. So, we'd bring our jacks with us. Papá promenaded past the refrigerator cases, pointing out cuts of meat and discussing with Mamá how that shoulder roast looked good, or why not a piece of stuffed flattened tenderloin? Agustín was already cleaning the braising steak that Mamá inevitably ordered, arguing that she did so because we liked it so much. But really, it was she who loved watching him lard it up with a long blade loaded with bacon and julienned carrots, which he stabbed into the meat and then extracted, clean as a toreador's sword after the death blow.

Come! Look, you two! Mamá said, as she tried to make us stop running around on the granite floor to share her delight in this ordinary task. Look!

We both admired Agustín's skill in wielding the broad, sharp knives and the slender ones he used to detach the fat and skin, which he then piled up and put aside for our grandparents' dog. He put those bits into a clear plastic bag that my sister and I would refuse to carry. It was Agustín's moist hands that had knotted the bag closed, and it was sticky. But Papá and Mamá achieved their maximum exaltation when, on top of a piece of tree trunk, Agustín hammered the slices of sirloin steak with a meat mallet until they were thin enough for beefsteaks, then flattened them out even more for the meaty thin fillets that Mamá served au gratin. "Winter Sheets," she called the recipe, insisting on preparing them that way even though Papá always scraped off the bubbling cheese. It detracts from the taste of the beef, he'd say. The two of them fell silent as the flat hammer pounded away and at last subdued the animal muscle. For them, Agustín was like a virtuoso percussionist. His rhythmic sounds accompanied us as we played jacks on the inside steps of the butcher shop, our safe zone between the mounds of animal chunks and the street where people and cars were passing by.

The nightmare continued at home when they ate the meat they'd just bought. Between bites, Papá graded the level of doneness of the meat, the age of the animal, the quantity of salt, the lack of tenderizing, the need for pepper or thyme. Mamá chewed with her eyes closed and then said she would complain to Agustín that the lamb was too old, that the greasy taste had given it away.

We wondered if their courtship had taken place in that arena of animal flesh. But no, Mamá said that on Saturdays they used to go to Ajusco to eat quesadillas. It all began when *you* were born, she said, pointing at me and smiling as if I were to blame for the whole business. We took you along in the stroller. What a horror, I thought, imagining myself snuggled into my pink pillows in the midst of all those pieces of cow, slices of pig, and tender, skinned lambs. When our grandparents came by on Saturdays to take us out for spaghetti, we welcomed them with grateful kisses. That day, anyway, my sister and I wouldn't have to eat those bloody rocks carved out by Agustín.

Just think, right now you're eating a little baby calf, Estela said to me maliciously when Mamá served us veal. The meat was quite soft, so we didn't have to work very hard to stick the chewed pieces under the tabletop. One day Lola counted them, furious about the putrid mess it was her job to clean up. We didn't speak to her for a few days. But after that, we had to swallow without complaint every single piece of the kilos of meat that appeared before us, entered our refrigerator, and struck our parents' fancy.

The Christmas season was the pinnacle of their obsession. Estela and I exchanged looks when Mamá gazed in delight at the marble-topped table that Papá had bought her, the precise thickness and rounded-off edges that would allow the two of them to give form and precision to hunks of muscle right there at home, just like Agustín did at the butcher shop. Papá sighed happily at the sight of his gift from her, a set of impeccably manufactured German knives. They wanted to try them out right away. When the butcher's dowry of gifts they could give each other seemed to be reaching its end, they teamed up to buy an electric meat grinder. They hurled fistfuls of meat into the spiky apparatus and looked on as white-streaked pink worms were extruded from its metal orifices. They looked like kids before a stolen treasure trove of candy canes. If Christmas fell on a Sunday, we were spared the trip to Agustín's. But they would drag us over there on the twenty-sixth because they were giving a sweater or a wallet to their partner in crime.

When Papá turned fifty, Mamá asked his friends to take him out partying the day before because she needed to install a butcher's block fashioned from a tree stump in the house, one that was nearly identical to Agustín's. They had to remove the kitchen door to wedge it in while Mamá shouted at us to come downstairs to see. By that time, Estela and I had managed to convince them to leave us at home or at the club on Saturdays, and the butcher shop had begun to fade into the shameful past of our childhood. But that tree trunk, in the dead center of the kitchen, was a fresh affront. What were we going to tell our friends when they came over to our house? Your Papá's a butcher, they'd say, mocking us. It's horrible, I said. Lola won't be able to cook, Estela chimed in. Mamá looked at the stump and, without paying the slightest attention to our objections, she proudly declared: Your father will be happy.

Indeed, on weekends our house was filled with that rhythm of Agustín's they admired so much, unmusical at first and then becoming metrical with practice. By then, they had started to buy larger chunks of meat so they could fillet them and flatten the cutlets themselves. Mamá laughed at Papá's clumsiness. At first, they didn't know what to do with so much flattened meat, nor did we know what to do with the monotony of the menu. But as time went on, they dreamed up new dishes and organized dinner parties with all their friends to whom they showed off their stump, the knives hanging on the kitchen wall, and that slab of marble which was already permanently bloodstained. Their friends were dazzled by their hobby because, outside of their workplaces, Papá's office and the university classrooms where Mamá taught, neither at the movie theater, at restaurants, nor on holiday, had anyone ever witnessed this degree of passion.

When Estela and I left home to begin our adult lives, we suspected those Saturday binges of buying and flattening meat were followed by cuddling sessions stimulated by the wine and food. Sometimes we'd ask each other, have you tried calling Papá and Mamá on Saturday afternoons? Because on that day of week, they never answered the phone to either one of us.

Mamá died before Agustín the butcher. Estela and I had joked innumerable times about what would happen to that weekend idyll if their mentor were to leave them. But we had never imagined that the butcher shop would first slowly lose its clientele and that, soon after, Mamá's sudden heart attack would leave Papá so very alone. He kept working, and on Saturdays he'd call a taxi to take him to the butcher shop. At first, he tried to go on as if nothing had happened. Lola was the one who kept us up to date. *Your Papá left utter mayhem in the kitchen*. We were comforted to imagine the blood still dripping from the stump, though Mamá was no longer around to wipe the floors down with a rag. We liked to visualize the meat mallet on the tree trunk. We insisted on taking him out to eat or inviting him to our homes, but he still clung to his Saturday ritual as always, until he lost his appetite and his friends stopped inviting him over to play dominoes and he no longer cared what was on his plate or even knew if it was Monday, Thursday, or the weekend. Life seemed to lose all meaning for him, and Papá became downhearted and hermit-like. The kitchen became Lola's exclusive domain, and she walked around the tree trunk there in the dead center of it and kept the marble tabletop clean, as if at any moment Papá might take up his meaty hobby again.

That's why sometimes on Saturdays now, I go and pick up Estela, and we park the car right in front of the butcher shop where Agustín no longer works. The newsstand is still right there where it always was. We walk down the stairs where we once played jacks and stand in front of the refrigerator cases. We order four or five kilos of beefsteak just so we get to hear the hammering of the meat mallet on the slab and Mamá's laughter. Then we go home with tears in our eyes and meat for the week.

Mónica Lavín (México, 1955) is the author of nine books of short stories, notably *Ruby Tuesday no ha muerto* (Gilberto Owen Literary National Prize, 1996); *Uno no sabe* (2003, Antonin Artaud award finalist); *La corredora de Cuemanco y el aficionado a Schubert* (Punto de Lectura, 2008), *Manual para enamorarse* (2011), *La casa chica* (Planeta: 2012). She has written ten novels including: *Café cortado* (Best Book of the Year, Premio Narrativa de Colima 2001); *La más faulera* (Grijalbo), a best-selling novel for young readers; *Despertar los apetitos* (Alfaguara, 2005); *Yo, la peor* (Grijalbo, 2009; winner, Premio Iberoamericano de Novela Elena Poniatowska); *Doble filo* (PRHM, 2014); *Cuando te hablen de amor* (Planeta, 2017), finalist for the Vargas Llosa Novel Award (2019) ; and *Todo sobre nosotras* (Planeta 2019) Her stories appear in anthologies both in Mexico and abroad, including in *Cuentos de ida y vuelta* (Editora Regional de Extremadura, 2020). She is a fellow at the Banff Centre for the Arts, Yaddo Colony of the Arts, and The Hermitage. She writes for El Universal and interviews for Public Television in Mexico. She is a member of Mexico's Sistema Nacional de Creadores and is a professor in the Creative Writing Department at the Autonomous University of Mexico City (UACM).

WIKIPEDIA ENGLISH: Mónica Lavín
WEBSITE: monicalavinescritora.com
TWITTER: @mlavinm

Dorothy Potter Snyder: writer, literary translator. Dorothy Potter Snyder writes short fiction and essays, and translates literature from Spanish. She is a passionate promoter of contemporary Hispanic women's texts. Her translations have appeared in *The Sewanee Review, Exile Quarterly, The Center for the Art of Translation, Review: Literature and Art of the Americas, Reading in Translation,* and *Two Lines Press,* among others. She is a contributor to *Public Seminar, Potent Magazine,* and *La Gaceta de Tucumán* (Argentina). Her original fiction has appeared in *The Write Launch, East by Northeast Magazine, Teresa Magazine,* and her short story in Spanish, *La puerta secreta,* was awarded a *mención honorífica* by the 2020 International Short Story Contest of the San Miguel Writer's Conference. A former New Yorker, she now lives in Hillsborough, North Carolina.

PERSONAL WEBSITE: DorothyPotter.com
TWITTER: @DorothyPS
FACEBOOK: Dorothy Potter Snyder
INSTAGRAM: dpsnyder_writer

Made in United States
Troutdale, OR
08/03/2024

21717746R00076